the Masquerade

the Masquerade

Sarah
Anne
Sumpolec

MOODY PUBLISHERS

CHICAGO

© 2003 by
SARAH ANNE SUMPOLEC

Library of Congress Cataloging-in-Publication Data

Sumpolec, Sarah Anne.
    The masquerade / Sarah Anne Sumpolec.
        p. cm. — (Becoming Beka series)
    Summary: When she moves to a new school Beka only pretends to be a
Christian, but when she learns that truth brings freedom, she gains
peace, faith, and friends.
    ISBN 0-8024-6451-3
    [1. Moving, Household—Fiction. 2. Friendship—Fiction. 3. High
schools—Fiction. 4. Schools—Fiction. 5. Christian life.] I. Title.

PZ7.S9563Mas 2003
[Fic]--dc21

                                                    2003007125

1 3 5 7 9 10 8 6 4 2

Printed in the United States of America

For my husband, Jeff—without him there would be no Beka.
And for Jesus Christ—without Him, there would be no me.

"I can't see. I'm going to have to stop again," I say. I pull over and scrape at the windshield with my glove. The drizzle is freezing as fast as it falls, so I get as much off as I can and then dive back into the warm car.

"Crazy night, isn't it?" my mother asks as she rubs my back quickly to warm me up. It doesn't really help, but it feels nice.

"Well, we don't have too much farther to go," I say, flashing a grin at her. Even bundled up in the parka she seems delicate. But it's her confident face that I admire most. No wonder half the town brings their kids to her office.

"Beka, honey, slow down up here. The road has probably gotten really icy." I carefully slow down, but the headlights coming towards me seem too close, maybe even on my side. I squint to see *better. The lights must be over the line. I swerve the car right to avoid a collision but can't get back on the road. My mother stiffens her legs against the floorboard as if she could stop the car from her side. We start spinning around and around. It feels slow. Then, the car slips off the embankment and starts tumbling down the hill, end over end. It feels like a carnival ride, except for the sound of metal being crushed and glass shattering.*

Then it stops. I listen but can't hear anything. I look at my mom. There is blood. Her eyes are closed. "Mom? Mom!"

*   *   *

Breathing heavily, and drenched in sweat, I sat up and clenched my blanket. When I saw where I was I lay back down, turned on my side, and waited for my heart to slow down. The dark windows told me it was still night even before I glanced at my alarm clock. Four A.M. I knew I wouldn't be going back to sleep.

The dream had been coming regularly, but now it was more like twice a week instead of once a month. It was always the same. Except sometimes I don't slow down the car. I closed my eyes and thought about my mother. In her white coat at the hospital. In her apron in the kitchen. I thought about her smile.

Shivering, I pulled the covers up closer. My heart ached, but I didn't cry. The tears wouldn't come. *I don't deserve to cry,* I thought. *If I had been a better daughter, she probably would still be here. She'd be downstairs right now sleeping next to my father. She'd get up in a few hours and make breakfast for all of us.*

But she wasn't here. She was dead. And I had to figure out life without her.

It's funny how, in your head, your memory tells you things were much better than they really were. In my memories we were close. We smiled at each other and understood each other's hearts. But if I'm honest with myself, that's more imagination than memory.

I wanted to know her better than I did. We hardly understood each other at all. Yes, my imagination was much kinder than my memory. Memories stuck in my heart like barbed wire—anytime I moved or thought too long, there they were, stabbing at me. I'll never know the feeling of her arms wrapped around my shoulders or her hand smoothing my hair. As if those things could ease the ache in my heart. Even if she were still here I would still be me. I couldn't seem to escape that.

She had been gone nine long months, but in some ways, it felt like it was yesterday. I tried not to think about it too much. I had plenty of other things I was supposed to be thinking about anyway. I glanced at the stack of college brochures on my floor. Now there was something I didn't want to think about. *How can I make a huge decision like that when I can't even face myself in the morning?*

I walked over and tried to pick up the stack, but they slipped, and one by one they thumped to the floor. With only a few left in my hand, I threw them towards the trash can. I couldn't seem to get anything right lately. I knew I was being foolish, and part of me thought that getting out of here, away from my family, school, and my memories, might be just what I needed. But I couldn't muster the energy to even start the process. The brochures only came because I signed some paper at school.

I picked up one from Mary Washington College and looked at the students on the cover. They looked happy and confident, comfortable even. I couldn't look like that on my best days, and there weren't many of those. See, what was the point of college? People go to college to get somewhere, make something of themselves. I just wanted to disappear.

Reluctantly, I went to my closet. I grabbed a dark red sweater, chose some jeans and a turtleneck. I had less than an hour to put on my face—my face that said, "Yeah, everything's just fine."

I walked over and sat on the floor by the long, narrow netting that hung from my ceiling. The first rays of sunlight splayed across the green carpeting my mother always told me I would regret choosing. And I did. But I couldn't bear to change it, and so it stayed along with the butterfly border that wound its way along the top of the wall.

"How are you guys doing?" I reached my hand in where the netting overlapped and held out my index finger. The smallest caterpillar obliged and crawled slowly into my hand. I pulled him out and up to my face. The striking yellow, black, and white stripes of his body rippled as he moved round and round my hand. His little legs barely touched my skin before they began moving again.

"What should I name you, little guy? Roscoe? Nah, you don't want to be a Roscoe. Maybe, well, I guess you could be a girl. Riley? Let's call you Riley. That'll work if you're a boy or a girl. I know you're hungry. I'm going to get you some fresh leaves before I go, okay?" I slipped Riley back into the netting and let him crawl onto the maze of twigs at the bottom of the tower. He joined his four brothers or sisters and headed for the last remaining leaf lying at the bottom.

When I reached the kitchen it was exactly as I had left it the night before. The house was so still. It was about the only time of day that it *was* still, what with five people in the house. I never used to be the first one downstairs. Mom was constantly calling up the stairs to get me out of bed. Now with the nightmares and insomnia, I had discovered that waking up at the crack of dawn wasn't all bad. It was actually kind of peaceful.

I loved our kitchen because it was so cozy, all decked out with soft greens and yellows nestled in the smell of warm bread and cinnamon. A large oak island with a cooktop dominated the left half of the room, while the table took up the right half. My mom had made the flowered curtains just the year before. "Aren't they cheery?" she had asked us. I agreed with her, even though I hadn't felt "cheery" in quite some time.

I started a pot of coffee for Dad, knowing that he would emerge soon, wanting his first cup. I made extra since Paul has taken to drinking coffee too. Dad keeps telling him it's a bad habit, but he doesn't fight him much on it. My brother Paul will be graduating in the spring and is going to college on scholarship in the fall. He's a fantastic baseball player, but he wants to be a doctor. He figures if they are willing to pay his way he will certainly let them, but his schoolwork would be his real priority.

"Will you make me breakfast, Beka?" I turned to see my eight-year-old sister catapult herself into the kitchen and fling her arms around my waist. Looking down at her reddish blonde hair, I couldn't help but smile. It was hard to stay sad when Anna was around. She looked at me with that toothless grin that made her even more impossible to resist.

"Sure, sweetie, what would you like?"

She paused, looking around the kitchen. "Can I have pancakes?"

Now it was my turn to pause. In my mind, I quickly ran down the ramifications of having pancakes. Everyone would want some, I was sure. However, even with making them and the massive mess that would have to be cleaned, it was probably early enough to pull it off. Besides, it would keep me busy.

"Okay, on one condition, though," I told her. "Run up to your room and put on your black tights. These are blue."

She looked down at her legs and gasped. "I didn't even notice," she said seriously. Then she turned and barreled up the stairs. Anna never did anything slowly. I giggled as I thought of her tearing through her drawers trying to find tights. Suddenly that black cloud swept over me. Mom used to help Anna lay out her clothes every evening with this private little game they played. I shook my head, pushing the thought away. It was not going to do me any good to think. I reached into the pantry and pulled out the Bisquick and began gathering the other ingredients.

Anna came down shortly and was very helpful as I

gave her directions. I heard the back door slam, and Paul appeared around the corner wiping his face with a towel.

"Early morning run?" I smiled tentatively, our argument the night before still ringing in my ears.

"As always," he said. "Are you going to save me some of those pancakes? I have to run up and shower."

"I will," Anna called from her perch on the stool, "but you'd better hurry or I'll eat them all up!"

"You wouldn't!" he said.

"Yessss," Anna giggled as he grabbed her in a big, sweaty hug and then dashed up the stairs.

"Anna, honey?" I said to her. "Could you go pull about three leaves off the plant in the foyer and take them up to the caterpillars?"

"Ohhh, I love feeding the little caterpillars. They're so cute!" Anna jumped off the stool. I could hear her running back up the stairs.

As she went up, I heard Lucy's voice. "Goodness, Anna, you better slow down or you're gonna get hurt." I gave the batter a few extra hard stirs and forced a smile onto my face.

"Good morning, Lucy! Why don't you sit down? You can have the first batch of pancakes. How does that sound?"

"No, thanks," she said as she slipped into one of the chairs. "I'm really not hungry." I studied her as she slumped in the chair, her head down and her straight auburn hair covering her face. Something was definitely wrong. But I wasn't sure if I should try to say anything. She had been a bit moodier than usual lately and seemed to pull away anytime I got close. As Paul entered the room, I silently motioned for him to work on the pancakes. He nodded, glancing at Lucy, and took over the skillet. I walked over and stood by her chair. She didn't move for a minute, but when she looked up at me I wished I had just kept making pancakes.

"Is there anything I can do?" I sat down in the chair next to her.

She shook her head.

"I know it's hard sometimes, but it's no use being sad. It's not going to make things any different, will it?"

She wrinkled her brow. "Please don't act like you know what I'm feeling. How could you when you hide in your room all the time and never talk to me? Look, I'm fine. Just leave me alone."

I sat back a bit stunned. "Well, I'm your sister. I was just trying to—"

"Sister?"

"Hey, Lucy, can you give me a hand?" Paul's voice interrupted before she could say anything else.

"Sure." She stood and went over to the stove where Paul was cooking. I could have heard their conversation if I had wanted to, but I didn't want to know.

I stood up and swallowed the lump in my throat. I was ticked. I should have said something different, but she had caught me off guard. Lucy and I started having problems even before Mom died, but it no longer just felt like a separation; it felt as if we were on different planets. And we were, I guess. Not because I was three years older, but because of Mom. Lucy had spent all sorts of time with Mom, while I tried to avoid her. They went places together and spent time together. It used to make my insides hurt when they would come home laughing and smiling with their arms around each other. I wanted that with Mom too. But every time Mom asked me to go somewhere, I said no. I couldn't be with her like Lucy. She might have discovered my secret if I spent too much time with her.

It bothered me that Lucy and I couldn't even have a conversation, but part of me just didn't want to care. I didn't want to constantly worry about what everyone else was thinking. It consumed my thoughts. *Can they see what I'm really thinking? What I'm really feeling?* It almost felt like if I let it out, all that anger and sadness, I might never get it back in. I took a deep breath, trying to push those feelings back inside. I had to get through the day. That's all I had been doing lately—trying to get through the day.

Paul looked up and caught my eyes. I tried to smile but ended up looking away, not wanting him to see what was going on inside of me. He had an uncanny ability to look right through me. I never could fool Paul. Luckily, Anna chose that moment to come downstairs, and we were all soon occupied with setting the table, pouring drinks, and finishing up the cooking.

"Well, well, well, the whole gang is up and ready to go. I am impressed," Dad said as he came through the door.

"Hey, Butterfly," Dad said as he kissed my cheek and squeezed my shoulders, the pet name making me feel close and distant all at the same time.

"Daddy! Daddy!" Anna called as she reached up her arms for him. "What's my name?"

"You know your name, silly girl," he teased.

"You know, my special name. You call Beka Butterfly and Lucy Princess and me . . ." She stopped, waiting for him to finish.

"Miracle. You're our little miracle." He squeezed her tight and she giggled. Even though I had seen them have that same conversation a million times, I had to get out of the room.

"I'm going to check on the caterpillars," I said to no one in particular and escaped to my sanctuary. I made sure the netting was secure and wasted a few moments straightening out the pale yellow quilt embroidered with the delicate butterflies I had always loved. I waited as long as I could, then trudged back down the stairs, wanting much more to return to my room and stay there all day. I wouldn't have to worry about what to say. Before I reached the last step, I was determined not to let anyone know how I was feeling. No matter what.

*   *   *

Only Paul was left in the kitchen. He stood at the back door waiting for me to gather my backpack and jacket. He was eerily silent. Even though I had my own car, I usually rode with Paul to school. Parking was a bear and it made it easier to take one car. Only today, I would have given anything to drive myself. We walked out to the car, our shoes crunching the light blanket of snow on the grass. It was the only break in the silence. I dreaded him asking me anything, and I tried to keep a thoughtful, but not sad, look on my face. It worked all the way to school, but then, as we were walking to the building, Paul stopped and faced me.

"Rebekah, you really need to find someone to talk to. I don't care who it is, but you can't just keep going on like this. It's like you haven't even faced the fact that Mom is gone. You keep hovering over Anna, you argue with Lucy, but nobody can talk to you about anything serious. You never talk about missing Mom or feeling sad. You blow us off if we ask how you're doing. If you keep everything inside and don't talk about it, Beka . . . you could, well . . . I don't know, I'm just afraid for you. You act like everything is fine, but you know it's not. It's like you're not even you anymore. I love you, Beka, and if you want to talk, I'm here." He gripped my shoulders with his hands and looked at me so fiercely that I nearly burst into tears. But I didn't. And after a few moments, he gave me a hug and turned and went into the building.

I felt absolutely frozen, like I just couldn't move. My mind was racing, replaying his words in my head. I dealt with Mom's death. I wasn't avoiding it, was I? I knew she was gone. I could feel that anger getting bigger inside me. He didn't know everything. I was doing fine. I didn't need to advertise what was going on to be okay.

I swallowed the rest of my tears and pushed everything he said aside. I still had seven hours of school to get through. I adjusted my backpack, stuffed everything down inside, and walked into Bragg County High School determined to be okay. Whatever that meant.

Already the halls were filled, and I plunged into the stream headed towards the lockers. Glancing at my watch I realized that I had nearly fifteen minutes before homeroom. I sighed. I really didn't want to see anyone or talk to anyone. I opened my locker and gathered my books for the first two periods, then headed for the auditorium. Not many people were at that end of the building early in the day, and I would get some privacy. Or so I thought.

As I turned the corner I walked straight into Gretchen Stanley. She is one of those beautiful, popular girls who walk around with their swarm all day. We have known each other since third grade, and up until my mother died, we got along fairly well. She was duly sympathetic at first, but after a few months she said she was getting "bored of my long face" and couldn't understand why I didn't "snap out of it." She began telling the other girls that I was milking my mother's death for sympathy and that she just wasn't going to play along anymore. She stopped speaking to me, and so did a bunch of the other girls. Except when they were being snotty and sarcastic. They would patronize me and treat me like I was ten, then laugh and walk away. I thought it would wear off, and I didn't really care so much at first. But lately, Gretchen had been simply ruthless in her sickeningly sweet comments, and they were making me downright angry. I was in no mood to talk with her today. I was too afraid that I might burst into tears.

"Excuse me. Sorry, Gretchen," I said quickly and tried to move past her and the swarm, but she actually grabbed my arm. For a brief moment I considered shoving her but figured that would just make things worse.

"Rebekah, how are you doing?" She spoke just as if she were talking to a puppy.

"I'm doing just fine." I mimicked her tone of voice back. She puffed up her chest, and I braced myself for a nasty remark. But none came. She seemed to change her mind and then actually smiled at me.

"You don't have to act like that. You stepped on my foot. The least you could do is give me a moment of your time."

"And why would you want a moment of my time?" I pulled my jacket up against my chest and waited. I couldn't figure out what she was up to.

"I was looking for you to find out if you want to do something with us."

I paused and studied her face. Was this a joke, or was she serious? I looked at the other girls. Chrissy and Mai looked bored and uninterested. Theresa looked nervous. But no one seemed like they were laughing about it.

"Do something? With you? I thought I was pathetic. Or something like that."

"Oh, please! That's ancient history."

"If you call last month ancient history, then I'm not sure we're speaking the same language, Gretchen."

She stomped her foot. "Why are you doing this? I just wanted to know if you'd audition with us. I'm being completely genuine. Really." She smiled. When I didn't respond she continued. "They are having auditions for the spring musical this Thursday and Friday, and since we are all trying out I thought you might want to also. They're going to do *Annie,* and Mr. Thompson is directing it." She sounded excited about it. I still couldn't figure out if she was for real. I wondered if she was planning some terrible joke to play on me or something.

"Why are you asking me? I mean, we haven't exactly been friends lately. I'm just curious," I said quietly.

"My gosh, Beka, why are you so paranoid?" she snapped. "I was just trying to help you get back in the swing of things—you know, rejoin the land of the living. I mean, it's about time, isn't it?" She brushed past me. The other girls leaped towards her, and they moved down the hall as a unit. I turned and ran for the auditorium.

As I sank down in one of the chairs I heard the homeroom bell ring. I didn't move. *Who cares about homeroom?*

Who cares about being on time? I was so tired of always doing exactly what I was supposed to do. I tried to swallow the tears, but they started falling down my cheeks anyhow. I didn't understand why I felt so awful. Nobody seemed to understand me. I replayed the conversation with Gretchen over and over. She probably was plotting something against me. Why else would she suddenly be nice after six months of put-downs? *Wow, I really am paranoid.*

It didn't make any sense, though. Nothing made any sense. And Paul. My mind wandered back to his words in the parking lot. He didn't understand me either. My stomach turned over as I thought about my brother. It hurt somewhere inside to know that he was thinking those kinds of things about me. I laid my jacket on the seat in front of me and put my head down. I just wanted to disappear.

I must have fallen asleep, because the next thing I knew a bell was ringing. And, according to my watch, it was the second period bell. I was really late. I gathered everything and ran to class, desperately trying to think of an excuse. I looked through the little glass window and saw Miss Hansen passing out papers. I did not want to walk in that room late. Miss Hansen had appointed herself the guardian of the clock, and I would have to endure a lecture in front of the whole room. I knew because I had witnessed that lecture countless times. I ducked under the window and headed for the bathroom. I didn't really think about how stupid that was until I actually walked in and looked at the rows of stalls and sinks. What was I supposed to do in there for forty-five minutes? There wasn't even anywhere to sit, except for the obvious, of course, which I was not going to do. I should have just stayed in the auditorium or left school entirely, but there was really nowhere to go. I dropped my backpack in the corner and slid down the wall holding my jacket. I was not having a good day.

Then a toilet flushed and I suddenly became aware of the sneakers in the last stall. *How am I going to explain this one?* I dropped my head and pretended to be extremely engrossed in the zipper on my jacket. I heard the water running, but after a few minutes of listening for the door to the hallway, I figured I had just missed it. I looked up and realized that the girl had not left the bathroom but was standing right in front of me.

"Can I help you or something? I mean . . . are you like sick or something?" She looked down at me with a strange expression. I couldn't think of a single thing to say, so I just looked up at her and bit my lip to keep my mouth from quivering. *Don't start crying!* For some reason, I always chose the most inopportune times to start crying.

I folded my arms around my knees and dropped my head as I felt the first tears fall across my cheeks. My mind was whirling with Paul and Gretchen and Mom. At some point I was aware that this girl was sitting next to me with her hand on my back. I fought the tears. They weren't going to do me any good. They couldn't change the way things were. So I kind of just sat there and breathed. In and out. In and out. I concentrated on that until the feelings were stuffed back inside and I could look up with no fear of the tears showing up again.

I studied the girl sitting next to me. She was small framed with masses of thick dark wavy hair pulled back gently from her face. Pretty too, in a tough sort of way.

"Why did you stay?" I asked her.

She shrugged softly. "I don't know. I guess I thought maybe you might want someone here."

"I'm Rebekah Madison. I don't remember seeing you before. Are you new here?" I was feeling pretty awkward and thought small talk might be easier than explaining what was wrong with me.

"My name is Lori, Lori Trent. Thursday was my first day but I spent last week taking all of these tests and stuff. Today is my first day of classes." She spoke softly and carefully, like she was studying me, wondering if I could be trusted. There was something different about her. Gretchen would have never put up with me sitting in the bathroom, and she certainly wouldn't have even pretended to be concerned. I decided, for no particular reason, to take a chance.

"Thanks for staying. I guess I just needed to clear my head, and I didn't much feel like going to class. It's been a hard morning." I paused and sighed. "Actually," I said carefully, "it's been a hard year."

"Well, I hope you are feeling a little better." She glanced down at her watch and then looked up at me. "Are you going to class?" I shrugged and dropped my head. "I have—" she paused and looked at a crumpled piece of paper that she pulled from her pocket, "English literature with Hansen. I think I'm pretty late."

I felt bad because I was the one who had made her so late. And it's not like she knew the teachers yet. I smiled at her and said, "That's my class too. Miss Hansen is really strict about being on time, but maybe we'll only be in half the amount of trouble if we walk in together."

She laughed and I noticed for the first time how beautiful she really was, like a china doll with small, perfect features and even white teeth. I had a feeling Gretchen was either going to draw her into the swarm or try to alienate her completely. Gretchen didn't do real great with other beautiful people. "That sounds like a good plan," she said. We gathered up our backpacks and headed towards class.

Miss Hansen gave us a brief lecture on respect and tardiness but allowed us to sit down without too much trouble. I sat in my usual seat, third row to the right of the room (if you're facing the blackboard). The only other empty seat was in the back of the room, and Lori quietly made her way to the back. I was sort of sorry that I couldn't sit near her. Even though I didn't know much about her, she interested me, and I thought it would be cool to get to know her.

As Miss Hansen turned to write the five steps to evaluating poetry on the board, I heard my name being whispered softly. I looked up and found Gretchen pointing to a note on the floor by my foot. I picked it up, thinking it couldn't possibly be for me, but there was my name neatly printed on the front of the folded paper.

> Beka—
> Meet me by the gym before lunch.
> I want to talk to you about Annie.
> –Gretch

I shook my head as I read it. What was it with this girl? I couldn't figure out why she was all of a sudden being nice. I heard my name again. Miss Hansen was so busy talking to the board she didn't even notice half the class was absorbed in whatever daily drama had gotten their interest. Gretchen looked at me expectantly. I nodded my head to tell her that I would meet her before lunch. After she had turned around to pretend to be a studious student, I turned around to see where Lori was. She caught my glance and smiled.

I raced out of the room after class to avoid Gretchen but didn't realize that I had ditched Lori in the process.

"Wait up, Rebekah." I heard a breathless voice behind me. "I wanted to ask you a question." I turned to see Lori running to catch up with me. I moved to the side of the hall so we could talk without being trampled.

"Everyone just calls me Beka. Rebekah sounds so formal," I said as I adjusted my backpack. I was still feeling pretty stupid about how I had acted in the bathroom, and I didn't really know what to say to her.

"Oh, okay. Well, I was sort of wondering about lunch. I mean, I've got B lunch and I thought if you had the same lunch maybe I could go with you." She dropped her eyes and said, "I really don't know anybody yet."

"Sure, I guess that's okay . . . I have to talk with someone right before lunch, but I could meet you by the cafeteria. Okay?" How could I say no? I felt like I should tell her that I wasn't exactly someone who could help her get to know the "popular" people, and I felt guilty for not wanting her to run with the "popular" group. But I supposed she would find that out soon enough anyway.

"That sounds great. I've got to get to my next class, so I'll see you later. Bye." She turned and was soon meshed with the crowd. *Maybe today isn't going to be as bad as I thought.*

"**Where have you** been?"
Gretchen demanded as I approached her. She motioned to a few girls standing near her to go away, shooing them as you would a fly that was bothering you. I rolled my eyes and wondered why people put up with her.

"I had to drop off some photos to the yearbook office. You don't have to be so testy . . . I'm only a few minutes late." I shifted my backpack and waited.

"Sorry. I'm not trying to be mean. I was just anxious to talk to you about *Annie* . . . I'm really excited about it." I was so startled by her apology that it took me a few moments to realize that she was actually talking to me like a human being and not a puppy.

"Yeah, I've been kind of wondering why you want me to try out." I couldn't imagine what had changed her song and dance. I was curious to find out.

"Well, that's why I wanted to talk to you. Alone. Chrissy and all of them—" she motioned towards the cafeteria "—are just so brainless half the time. I guess I'm just bored. You and I used to get along, and I was sort of hoping we could be friends again. When I heard about the play I thought of you in a second and figured it would be so much fun to hang out together while we're working on it. I just forgot to ask you until now."

"Gretch, I don't get it. Why are you being nice? Why are you suddenly so interested in being friends with me?" I paused. I wanted to say more, but I could hear my voice cracking and didn't want to start crying again.

"How many times do I have to say I'm sorry? I'm over it. I was a jerk. Can't we just forget about it? It's getting really old anyway, and I miss having someone I can talk to. Satisfied?"

"I guess so, Gretch." I paused. "I just never know when to believe you." I wasn't sure that she had heard me, because when I looked at her, she was staring down the busy hall towards the cafeteria. I followed her gaze and saw Lori leaning against the wall to the left of the doors. Her arms were folded across her books, and she looked uncomfortable. I wondered how long she had been waiting.

"I better go. When are the auditions?" I asked.

"Thursday and Friday; callbacks are on Monday." She was still staring down the hall, but after a moment she turned slowly towards me and looked hard at me. "I hope you're not planning to be friends with that new girl. I caught her making eyes at Jeremy this morning. Who does she think she is anyway? You don't just waltz in the door and put the moves on my boyfriend."

"I thought he was your ex-boyfriend."

"That's only temporary. She's trouble, Bek. I certainly hope you take my advice." She shifted her backpack and tossed her short blonde curly hair. "Meet me and the girls after school tomorrow. The stage is supposed to be open for us to practice. Pick out a song to sing and Bruce can play for us. Okay?"

"Yeah, sure. Look, I gotta go. See ya." I hurried off down the hall to meet Lori. I was still trying to figure out what I should do about everything when she saw me coming. Her face cracked into a wide smile.

"I thought you weren't going to make it."

"Sorry, I had to talk with someone, and I didn't think it was going to take that long."

"Oh," she said quietly. I could tell she wanted to ask more, but she didn't. "Well, I'm pretty hungry. How's the food here?"

"Not too horrible. But I don't have much to compare it to. I really didn't eat here until last year—well, I mean last school year, more like since March of this year." I felt all flustered. Why did the weirdest things stir up all my emotions? Just because Mom used to pack my lunch until she died, here I was ready to cry in the middle of a hot, loud cafeteria in the middle of the day. Was I ever going to remember without it hurting so much?

Thankfully, Lori didn't ask any more questions, and lunch was pretty uneventful. I was so glad that Gretchen wasn't there. She has the lunch period right before me. I found out more about Lori. I found out she had a six-year-old sister named Kari Lynn. I told her about my brother and sisters, and she thought that was pretty cool. Then she said she always wanted to have a brother or a sister, which I thought was strange because she had just told me she had a sister. But the lunch bell rang and we both had to make a mad dash for our next class, and I didn't get to ask her what she meant.

By the time I got home I really didn't feel much like doing anything. And I especially did not want to think about school. I still didn't trust Gretchen, but it sure would be nice to have friends again. I had been without them for so long, I had forgotten what it was like to not be lonely. And then there was Lori. She seemed really nice and she was fun to talk to, but it was obvious that Gretchen was not going to be very accepting. I knew as soon as I saw Lori that she would pose a real threat to Gretchen, but I didn't understand Gretchen's comments about Jeremy. If anything, Jeremy was probably the one who was making eyes at Lori, not the other way around. Regardless, it was just one more thing to worry about.

And then there was *Annie* to consider. It would make Paul and Dad happy to see me involved with something again, but for some reason, I couldn't get excited about it. But it wouldn't hurt to try out either. Gretchen seemed sincere enough, and it might be just the thing to get my mind off everything else. I had managed to borrow a copy of the script from the library and was sort of anxious to curl up with it and see what the play was like.

I walked through the kitchen and immediately

noticed that Mary wasn't there making dinner. *That's odd,* I thought. Dad had hired Mary to help keep house, and she usually made dinner for us on weeknights. Then I saw it. Before I even picked it up, I knew what it was going to say. I clenched my teeth in irritation as I read.

Beka,
Your father asked me to leave this note for you.
Please cook the spaghetti for dinner. Everything you need is on the counter or in the icebox.

Thank you, Mary

The note didn't say why she couldn't be there, and the longer I stood looking at it, the angrier I got. If I made dinner and cleaned up, I wouldn't even be able to start my homework until after dinner, which left very little time to read the play. Why did I have to pick up the slack? The play was due back at the library in the morning because so many people wanted to see it. I crumpled up the note and threw it into the trash and considered my options. I shrugged and headed to my room. If anyone asked, I'd just say I never got the note. I went back and dug the note out of the trash, took it to my room, and tore it into tiny little pieces. It wasn't fair anyway.

I decided to get my homework done right away so I could concentrate on the reading and was so deeply engrossed in my trig homework that I jumped when someone pounded on my door.

"Beka, are you in there?" I heard my dad's deep voice. I glanced at my watch. It was already 6:30, and suddenly a wave of guilt washed over me. Dad had probably just gotten home and seen that there was no dinner ready. Reluctantly, I invited him in.

"Mary called me at the office earlier to tell me that there was an emergency with her mother. You know that she has been sick lately." He paused as if expecting an answer. I looked up for a moment and nodded my head but couldn't keep looking at his eyes. I looked away.

"Well, she said she would leave a note asking you to get dinner ready." Another long pause, and then he asked, "Did you get the note?"

Wow. What was I supposed to do now? It was so easy a few hours ago to think that I was going to just lie about it if anyone asked, but that seemed so much harder now with my father standing there staring at me. The guilt was overwhelming, and then I began to get angry again. Most everyone I knew lied to their parents. I had lied to them for years. What was wrong with me? Then I started thinking about how it wasn't fair to always expect me to do what I shouldn't be expected to do. I hardened my face. "I didn't see any note. I rushed upstairs to do my homework right after school." At least that part was true. I comforted myself with the fact that I only half lied.

He paused, and for a moment, it looked like he was going to respond. Then he turned and walked towards my door. He looked back as he was leaving and said, "I guess I can have something ready in about half an hour, so come down around seven, okay?" He didn't wait for my answer, and the door shut softly behind him. Half of me felt like celebrating, like I had won by successfully lying and doing what I wanted to do no matter what. The other half felt like there was lead at the bottom of my stomach. It bothered me that it bothered me. It wasn't fair, so why was I feeling guilty?

When Lucy came up a little after seven to remind me to come down to dinner, I yelled, "I can tell time. I'm not four. I'm just not coming down, so leave me alone." She looked so surprised and hurt that I wanted to apologize as soon as the words left my mouth. But she closed the door and I could hear her running down the steps.

I sat there stunned that I could be so mean. But why couldn't everyone just leave me alone? Paul, Gretchen, Dad . . . I had enough to deal with. And I knew what time it was. Lucy didn't have to come and remind me like I was Anna. My stomach growled. But I wasn't about to go downstairs after I had acted like that. They could just sit down there and figure it out for themselves that I wanted to be left alone. No one understood.

I waited until the last possible
moment to go downstairs the next day, and fortunately
everyone but Paul had left. Paul followed me outside,
and on the back porch I turned and told him I was driving my own car. He did not seem pleased with my little
announcement. "Well, I'm not going to stop you or anything, but I kind of wanted to talk with you about a couple
of things on the way to school. I'd appreciate it if you'd
ride with me."

Suddenly, I remembered that I had a great excuse not
to ride with him. "I have to stay after school today; I
promised Gretchen I'd . . ." I stopped, realizing that I
didn't want him to know that I was going to try out for

the play. I didn't bother finishing the sentence because Paul was just staring at me.

"I'm sure Gretchen or someone else can give you a ride home, or you can call and I'll pick you up."

"Fine then," I growled at him. "You just have the answers to everything, don't you?" He ignored my sarcasm and unlocked the car. I threw in my backpack to show him I was angry in case he had missed it. I sat there and fumed.

"What are you so upset about this morning?" he asked gently, and for one weak moment I wanted to just let it all out. I felt something like a dam holding back water. If I broke, I'd never get all that water back in. So I sat back in the seat, stared straight ahead, and said, "Nothing."

"Yeah, right nothing. You're not a very good liar." I shot him a nasty look and resumed my staring-straight-ahead position. Even as I was resisting telling Paul anything, I was getting more confused than ever about my own feelings. I felt so out of control all of a sudden, and it was kind of scary to not understand what was going on inside of me.

"Well, anyhow, I needed to ask you a favor. Dad has got a business meeting tonight and Mary has to leave early, so it's up to you and me tonight. Now you can have the choice. You can either take Lucy to youth group at church or stay with Anna."

"Why do I have to do either? Can't you just take Anna with you when you take Lucy to youth group?" I tried to ask normally, but my voice revealed my annoyance.

Paul sighed loudly. "Can't you just help out? You

know someone has to stay with Lucy because it is pointless to drive her out there and drop her off, because by the time you drive home, you basically have to turn around and drive back again to pick her up."

"Fine, fine then, I'll stay home with Anna. It's not like I have a life or anything important like that." I wanted to stay as far away from that youth group as possible. I was not up to facing all of them. I'm sure they knew far more about me than I was comfortable with. After all, Lucy had been going for a long time. The fact that I refused to go was a sore point even before Mom died. I turned and looked out the window and tried not to think about all the memories that were surfacing inside of me. My nose and eyes began to burn, and, desperate to keep from crying, I began to mentally list all the songs I knew. I had forgotten last night to come up with something for the audition.

Paul didn't say anything else, and before long he swung into the parking lot. He closed his door and walked quickly to the building, leaving me standing there in the parking lot. He didn't even say good-bye. It hurt. Paul and I used to be close, but this wall felt like it was ten feet tall. It upset me to know that it was probably my fault. I felt trapped though, like I didn't even know how to stop being angry, much less explain it. I walked slowly into the building. I still had the whole Gretchen versus Lori thing to deal with, and I still didn't know what to do about that.

Fortunately, I did not run into either of them right away. Lori and Gretchen were both in my second period English class with Hansen, and since I had been late yesterday, I made sure that I was there early to redeem myself. The last thing I needed was to get in trouble at school. I slid into my seat and opened my books just as Lori walked into the room. She grinned when she saw me, which sort of annoyed me. Why had she latched on to me? She slid into the chair next to mine and said, "I told Megan about you last night, and she wants to know if you could come over to dinner tonight. I think she wants to meet you and thank you for being nice to me. It's kind of dumb, but I promised her I'd ask you." She looked at me expectantly, trying to cover up her eagerness.

"Who's Megan?" I asked, looking at her curiously.

"Oh," she said and dropped her head. "I mean my mom. I mean, well, she's . . . I call her Megan." She glanced back up and caught my still-confused expression, but I just shrugged, figuring it wasn't the time or place to ask more questions.

"Yeah, I'm sure that would be fine." Actually I thought it would be great because that meant one more dinner I didn't have to face at home. And then I remembered Paul. "Oh, bother, I forgot. I can't come tonight because I promised my brother I'd watch my sister."

"Oh, well, maybe you can come tomorrow night, if you want to."

"That'd be fine." I smiled. She did seem really nice. My annoyance had passed and I found myself looking forward to tomorrow night. Then maybe I'd understand her home situation. The bell rang and I faced Miss Hansen and her droning voice, which made even poetry sound boring.

Gretchen had not been in second period and I was

wondering if she was absent or what. I had been working up my enthusiasm about the play but was really nervous about practicing with Gretchen's clan. I couldn't decide if I wanted her to be there or not. By seventh period I had my answer. Gretchen waltzed into journalism class late and tossed a note on my desk as she went by.

Bek—
The rehearsal is still on. I had to miss the first half of school for a doctor's appt. Can I get your 2nd period notes? Meet us by the theatre after the last bell.
                                                                          -Gretch

The first half of journalism is like a regular class, but the second half we get to break up and work on the school newspaper, *The Bragg About.* We put it out monthly, or at least we try to. Ms. Adams is our advisor and is definitely one of my favorite teachers, and journalism is my favorite class. When we split up, I settled in to finish my story about the new computers that were donated to the school. I was working intently, so when Gretchen suddenly appeared at my desk, I jumped.

"Did you read my note?" she asked.

"Yes, I did." I thought it was fairly obvious I'd read a note that she dropped directly on my desk.

"So, are you coming or what?"

I gave her a dirty look and said, "I told you yesterday that I would come."

She grinned at me, "Well, Miss Attitude. That's a switch." She laughed and said, "I just wanted to make sure you didn't change your mind."

"No, but I don't really know what to sing. I didn't get a chance to pick something out."

"Oh, don't worry about that. I brought all my music and you can look through it this afternoon." She lowered her voice and said, "I know we used to get along, but we never really hung out before or did a lot of things together. You seem different now—cooler I guess. Like you won't be such a prude about doing things with us now that your mom is gone." She paused. "Don't take that the wrong way; I just mean that it seems we'll be able to do more stuff together."

I didn't quite know how to react to her statements but, in a way, she was right. When Mom was around, I didn't accept the offers to go to parties and stuff because I thought I'd disappoint her. Now, I didn't really care what I did, as long as I didn't stay still. When I stayed still I thought too much.

"Anyhow," she said quickly, "I'll see you after school." She swaggered off and joined Chrissy and Mai at the computers. After she left, I had a hard time focusing on my story. *Was I a prude before?* I thought back to when Mom was around. I had thought I was like everyone else, except for the religion thing. Did it affect school that much that people had thought of me as a prude? I tried to remember what I did with school kids before Mom died and I couldn't remember much apart from a couple of clubs and having one or two friends over. Celia, who had been my best friend, moved away a few months before Mom died. I almost laughed as I remembered how devastated I was when she moved away. I had thought it was the end of the world, but she only moved a few hundred miles away, whereas my mom was gone forever. I sighed as that dark cloud moved in over my thoughts.

I loved my mother, but we had our mother-daughter difficulties. I suppose all moms and daughters do. But I never got the chance to work things out with her, you know, to make things right. When I was about eight, and Mom was pregnant with Anna, she and Dad went away for a week. Paul, Lucy, and I went to stay with our grandparents in Maryland. Well, when they came to get us they were different. Different in a weird way. They explained that they had gone to a marriage conference so they could grow closer together. Apparently, it had been recommended by some of their acquaintances.

I remembered being worried because I thought they were going to get a divorce. The pregnancy had been difficult and they were fighting endlessly. I had never heard of anyone going away to a conference about marriage. They sat us all down and told us they had become born-again Christians and that they were going to live their lives for God now. It made no sense to me. We suddenly all had our own Bibles and we started going to church every Sunday. A new church. We never went back to the church we had gone to every Christmas and Easter. We started having dinner together and right after dinner we all had to do devotions. Daddy would read a passage from the Bible and then talk to us about it.

I never really knew what to think about all the changes. I never said much, and I never really liked church and devotions and youth group like everyone else. I thought something was wrong with me, and the more

I felt that way, the harder it was for me. I felt like I wasn't really part of the family anymore, because they all had this common bond that I just couldn't catch on to. Over the years, Paul, Lucy, and even Anna had all "accepted the Lord" and were "saved." They all got baptized in the lake by our pastor, and everyone was all gooey, gushy happy about it. I remembered feeling physically sick when Anna got baptized, because I couldn't help but wonder what everyone was thinking about me. I was sure my mom thought something was dreadfully wrong with me.

On Sundays, after lunch, Mom would take us girls to the den and we would have a Bible study, while Dad took Paul. Well, those made me extremely uncomfortable, and I started making excuses. Any and every excuse I could come up with to keep from going into that den. Mom came up to my room one day and told me if I didn't want to do the Bible study, she wasn't going to force me. She seemed so sad and hurt, that I didn't know what to say to make things better between us.

That's when I started pretending to be a Christian. That night, as she sat on the edge of my bed, I started crying that I wanted to pray to be saved. I had been going to church and youth group long enough to know what other people did. I watched my mother's face light up like she had with everyone else. Tears streamed down her face as she told me how she had prayed for me and that the angels were rejoicing in heaven for me. I cried too, but not because I was happy like my mom, but because it wasn't the truth. I closed my eyes as she prayed for me and tried desperately to figure out how to tell her that I really wasn't ready. She held my hands and told me to repeat the prayer after her. But I really didn't. I just mumbled under my breath to make it sound like the words she was saying.

Later, after she cried and hugged me for a while, she took me downstairs and told everyone what had happened. Then everyone was crying and hugging, and I sank deeper into a despair that I didn't know how to fix. Then the real acting began. I endured the whole church and youth group thing with a half smile on my face, while whispering to myself that I was a liar.

The water baptism was the hardest. I guess I always thought there was a God, but that day at the lake I was sure that I was going to go to hell. He knew that I had lied, and I couldn't bear to face Him. But after the initial reaction, things died down after a while. I stopped getting those pitying looks from my family and the people at church who knew I hadn't accepted the Lord, and everyone suddenly relaxed about me. I guess they thought if my soul was saved then I was going to be okay. But I wasn't. I did all the stuff that I was expected to, but I never meant it. I played the perfect daughter routine (which probably explained Gretchen's prude comment), and when we prayed, I'd scrunch up my eyes and pray that no one would find out. Especially my mother.

The only thing I couldn't handle was the Sunday afternoon Bible study with Mom. I just knew that she would find out about me if I kept going. So what I did instead was come up with new excuses not to go. Every time my mother approached me about it, I'd smile and tell her not to worry, that I was still going to youth group, Sunday school, and church, not to mention the dinner devotions. She smiled and told me that she just wanted me to be a part of the mother-daughters group because it was such a special time to really come to know each other. Which was exactly why I couldn't bear going. So, for three years I masqueraded as a Christian.

Then she was killed in that car crash. The guilt I had been feeling for years suddenly tripled in one afternoon. I couldn't face anyone, especially God, and after that I stopped everything but church. I couldn't get out of Sunday mornings. No one really said anything about it. I guess nobody wanted to pressure me after Mom died. But all of that guilt inside of me mixed with an anger that I didn't understand. I couldn't even figure out who I was angry with—my mom, my family, myself, God? Everything had recently begun to irritate me. Especially my family. They all cried and hugged and loved all over each other after Mom died, and I just couldn't pretend to be a part of that. I'd go to my room and everyone pretty much left me to myself. But they were all moving on now, with only a few tears here and there.

For a long time, I couldn't cry about it. I didn't feel like I deserved to be able to cry like everyone else. Guilt and anger had become such a deep part of my life by then that I just figured this is how it would always be. But instead of subsiding, things were getting more confusing. I felt guilty that I had lied for so long, angry that God took her away, sad that I couldn't fix things now, and angry that everyone knew my mother but me. She always said that now that I was saved, we were closer than even mother and daughter. But the closer she got to me, the farther I'd move away for fear of my secret being let out. So, I purposely shut my mother out from knowing me, and because of that, I never knew her like everyone else did. And now I never would.

"I didn't know that computer article was going to be so moving."

I jumped and looked at Ms. Adams, who was kneeling by my desk. I could feel the tears running down my cheeks, and I quickly brushed them away and stood up.

"Are you okay, Beka?" She looked really concerned as she rested a hand on my shoulder.

"Yeah, sure," I said quickly. "Can I go to the rest room?" Ms. Adams nodded and I quickly went to the bathroom and tried to clean myself up. I waited until no one could tell I had been crying. As I took one last look in the mirror, I whispered, "I hate you!" and walked out to face the rest of the day.

After the final bell, I went
to my locker and put away the junk I didn't need and
gathered up my books for homework. I was stalling. I
was all of a sudden very nervous about this rehearsal.
How did I get myself into this? I was glad that Gretchen had
apologized and everything, but all those other girls had
been nasty too. Maybe it would be okay. Since Gretchen
was in charge, I could only hope the other girls would be
pleasant as well. Unless there really was something to be
paranoid about. I sighed and scolded myself for getting
all worked up over nothing.

I started towards the auditorium when I ran into
Lori. She smiled when she saw me.

"Hey, how are things going?" I asked.

"Not too bad. The teachers seem nice and all. I suppose it'll just take some getting used to. I'll check with Megan tonight to see if tomorrow is okay for you to come over to dinner." She paused and caught my glance. "That is, if you still want to."

"Sure," I said quickly. "I'd like to meet your family."

She looked away as her eyes filled with tears. I only caught a glance, but she seemed really upset. "Is something wrong?"

She shook her head without looking up. "No, it's just that I really don't want anybody to know." She then lifted her head and looked me dead in the eye. "Except you. Can I trust you? I feel like I can but . . ." Her voice trailed off.

I was startled by her emotion and pointed question. Could she trust me? Could anyone really trust me after I had betrayed my family and lied about who I was? *Well,* I thought, *I kept my secret pretty well.*

"Absolutely, if you mean about not telling anyone at school."

"That's pretty much what I mean."

"So, what is it? What did I say that upset you?"

She shook her head, "Not now. Not here. I'll tell you all about it tomorrow night, 'kay?"

"As you wish," I said, giving her a slight bow. She laughed and it sort of lightened the mood.

"Are you going home? I thought the cars were this way," she said, pointing behind me, "but I'm still getting turned around in here. Am I going in the wrong direction?"

I took a deep breath. Now what could I say? If I told her about the little rehearsal, would I rope myself into having to invite her? It wouldn't have been a problem, except that Gretchen had already clearly stated her feelings. And I didn't want to hurt Lori's feelings either.

"Well," I said carefully, "I'm meeting some people after school to practice some songs."

"Oh," she said. "Is it for the tryouts for the musical? I saw some posters for it today. What is it, *Annie?*"

"Yeah, I sort of gave my word that I would do it." She stood quietly as if trying to figure out what to do. "Are you going to try out?" I figured I would just get it over with.

"Oh, goodness no. I'm not singing in front of anything except maybe my bathroom mirror."

I laughed with relief. I didn't have to hurt anybody's feelings. We made quick good-byes and agreed to talk during lunch the next day.

*　　　*　　　*

When I entered the auditorium, the first thing I heard was Gretchen barking orders at the others up onstage. I made my way slowly up the aisles and stopped at the orchestra pit. I shifted uncomfortably as I waited for Gretchen to see me. I didn't have to wait long.

"Hey, Madison," she called from the stage. "Come on up here and look through the music with Theresa." She shot a dirty look at the red-haired girl sitting on the floor. "She didn't come prepared either."

I quickly joined Theresa on the floor and gave her a

smile. She seemed relieved that I wasn't going to yell at her, and I said quietly, "I thought Thompson was directing it. Who left Gretchen in charge?"

She laughed and put her hand over her mouth as she looked up at Gretchen, who was completely oblivious.

"Well," I said, sighing, "we better find something." We divided the stack of books in half and began going through them. Many of the songs were familiar to me because I adored show tunes, especially the newer stuff, which Gretchen seemed to have a lot of.

As Theresa and I looked, Gretchen moved everyone into the auditorium so each girl could practice alone on stage. Theresa and I moved into the right wing, where Gretchen couldn't see us. Gretchen's brother Bruce had most likely been coerced into playing the piano for us. He was a freshman this year and seemed really talented. Lizzy stood quietly in the center of the stage and waited for Bruce to begin.

I went back and forth from listening to the others to sifting through the music. I finally settled on "Nothing" from *A Chorus Line.* I had always liked the song, but it seemed like I understood it better now. It talked about an emptiness inside the soul—where there was nothing. It was a pretty good description of how I felt.

As soon as Theresa finished her rendition of "Send in the Clowns," Gretchen bellowed my name from the auditorium. I gave Theresa a smile as she exited the stage and reappeared in the auditorium a few moments later. I handed Bruce the music and he took it without looking at me. He seemed kind of annoyed by this point, and I could hardly blame him since it was nearly five.

"What did you pick out?" Gretchen asked.

I told her what I had chosen and she groaned, "Someone else is bound to do that one. It's so typical for an audition."

"I really don't care; I like the song and that's that."

"Fine, have it your way, but don't blame me if ten other people do the same song." She waved at Bruce and sank into one of the chairs.

I practiced the song several times, as Gretchen and some of the others gave me some ideas on hand motions and movements. They had lots of good suggestions, and by the time we were done, I was pretty excited about auditioning and already fantasizing about getting a good part. Maybe even a lead. Why not? I figured I had as much of a chance as anyone else.

I took a deep breath and asked Gretchen for a lift home. "Paul brought me to school, so I don't have my car," I explained.

"I guess so," she said with a shrug as she walked down the stairs. "Let's go."

Fortunately for me, she also gave Mai and Theresa a ride home so I didn't have to talk. My enthusiasm for the play dwindled as we neared my house. I really didn't want to go home. I had become so tired of trying to figure out who I was supposed to be. Not to mention that I still felt like I was from a different planet than the rest of my family. As I lugged my backpack up the porch stairs, I tried to plan a strategy, but I couldn't figure out what to say to everyone. Then I started getting mad at everyone because I felt so uncomfortable going into my own house. When I came through the kitchen door, I threw it open and let the storm door slam behind me. The noise was strangely satisfying, and I felt even better when I slammed the door closed too.

"Oh, it's you. How are you doing, Miss Rebekah?" Mary asked quietly as I came out of the mudroom. She didn't mention the door slamming.

"Fine," I answered without looking up. I went straight through the kitchen and was halfway up the stairs before I realized I hadn't even asked how Mary's mother was doing. Part of me wanted to go back downstairs and apologize for being rude, but then I thought, nobody seemed to care how I was really doing, so why should I care about anyone else?

I sat down to work on my history homework, and before long there was a tiny knock at my door.

"Come in," I called, and the door opened quietly. Anna poked her head around the door.

"You comin' to dinner tonight?" she asked.

"Yeah," I said, sitting up. "What's the matter?"

"Nothing," she shrugged. "I just didn't know if you were going to yell at me like you yelled at Lucy last night. She was cryin' when she came to dinner."

My heart sank. I hadn't meant to hurt Lucy, and now I had even hurt Anna in the process.

"Come here for a minute, sweetie," I said as I held out my arms. She crawled into my lap and leaned her head against my shoulder. I squeezed her small body. I didn't want her to be scared of me. "Anna, you're my sister and I love you. Don't you ever forget that."

"Don't you love Lucy too?" she asked as she looked into my eyes.

"Sure I do. I just wasn't having a very good day. I shouldn't have yelled at her," I tried to explain.

"Didja ask her to forgive you?" Anna asked. "That's what Mama would have done."

"I know that," I said sharply. Anna pulled away from me and quietly stood up. She walked out the door without another word, but her silence was screaming at me. Why did I speak to her like that? Especially since she was right. That's exactly what Mom would have done. But I didn't want to ask Lucy to forgive me. I hadn't meant to hurt her feelings, so I really didn't do anything wrong. It's not like I punched her or something.

I walked slowly down the stairs to dinner. Everyone looked up as I walked into the room, but no one said anything. Dad motioned for us to hold hands as he said the prayer. As Lucy took my hand she whispered, "I forgive you," just as Dad began to pray.

"Heavenly Father, we thank You for this food that You have provided for us, and I thank You for each of the precious children gathered around this table. Help us all to grow in the grace and knowledge of our Lord Jesus Christ and to glorify You with our lives. Please bless this food and sanctify it for our bodies' health. In Jesus' name we pray, Amen."

Outside I said, "Amen," but on the inside I was seething. I hadn't asked Lucy to forgive me. I hadn't done anything wrong. As my family chatted about the day and laughed, I fumed. I felt so alone.

CHAPTER 6

It was my night to wash the dinner dishes, so that kept me occupied and I didn't have to talk to anyone. I scrubbed the dishes extra hard as I thought about everything. I stole several glances at Lucy. She looked so happy as she played with Anna on the living room floor. She was smiling and laughing, which annoyed me even more. Why was she so mopey yesterday? Why was it so wrong for me to have a bad day every now and then? The angrier I got, the harder I scrubbed.

As I shut off the water, I felt two heavy hands on my shoulders. I turned and looked up at Dad. He didn't say anything at first, and I was struck for a moment by how strong and handsome he looked. But his eyes looked sad.

"Beka, I'm a bit concerned about you lately. You've been snapping at the girls and being rude. I know that you are probably just having a difficult time with something and taking it out on us, but I would prefer you would talk with me or Paul or even Lucy, instead of acting out your feelings. Can you try to talk to someone for me?"

"I've just had a couple of rough days. I'm fine and I don't need to talk to anyone. I even made a new friend at school, and she wants me to come to her house for dinner tomorrow. I can't be that messed up if I can manage to make friends, can I?"

"I never said you were messed up, Beka. Your mood swings are just concerning me, and I don't want anyone to get hurt. I love you very much. Everyone needs someone to confide in . . . even you." He smiled warmly and gave me a hug. I could feel the stiffness in my own body and I just couldn't relax into his arms. He must have noticed because he straightened up quickly.

"Beka, I'd like you to take Lucy to youth group tonight and stay with her." He put one finger to my lips as I began to protest. "I know that you and Paul decided that he would go, but I would prefer that you take her. Paul isn't feeling very well and I think he should stay home and rest."

"Whatever," I said reluctantly. I knew he wasn't going to back down. I was sure that Paul and Dad had concocted this scheme to get me to that church. And I was going to have to be in the car with Lucy. It was going to be a long night.

*   *   *

Dad rushed off to his business meeting and Lucy was waiting in the kitchen, her Bible and notebook tucked under her arm, when I came down from my room. Lucy smiled widely at me as I walked past her out the back door. I just ignored her. Who did she think she was anyway?

The drive out to the church was really quiet, and I kept running over the day in my head. I knew I was being a total crab, but I felt like I didn't have the energy to change my own mood. It just took so much effort lately to be pleasant. I thought about Dad's words in the kitchen. He would be so disappointed in me if he knew the truth. About all my lies, about pretending to be something I'm not. I felt like I had been pretending so long that I really didn't even know who I really was. Lucy sat next to me with her Bible open on her lap. Even though we were in the same car, and from the same family, I felt like we were worlds apart. I couldn't come up with a single thing to say to try and break the ice. So I just kept quiet and choked back the tears. Dad was right; I really did want someone I could talk to, someone who could help me understand how to get out of this horrible cobweb I had created for myself.

*   *   *

The church was a nondenominational one, and services were held in what was once a grocery store. A lot of people were already there when I pulled the car into the parking lot. Several clusters of teenagers were standing around outside talking and laughing. Lucy jumped out of the car almost as soon as I stopped. And I sat there, trying to figure out what to do. I gathered up my school-books, and as I closed the door, out of the corner of my eye I saw someone headed right for me. I had nowhere to escape to.

"Beka, I'm so glad you came tonight! We haven't seen you in quite a while. How are you doing?" Her words tumbled out as she smiled broadly, almost too broadly. Her name was Susan Matthews and she was one of the adults who led the youth group meetings. I never liked her much even when I was coming to the meetings regularly. She asked too many questions and just acted too nice. I never believed she cared two hoots about me. I always got the feeling that she really didn't want to know how I was doing . . . she just expected me to say "fine" like everyone else. I think she would have fallen apart if someone actually said, "Well, to tell you the truth, my life stinks right now, and I don't want anyone trying to cheer me up!" It would have probably been funny to see her face though.

"Actually, I only drove Lucy. I have some homework to do." I forced a smile and ignored the "how are you" question.

"Oh," she said as her face fell. "I was hoping you were going to join in the meeting tonight. We have a guest speaker. It should be really good."

She seemed really sincere, and for a brief moment I wanted to trust her. But she knew my family, and I wasn't about to spill my guts to someone who might say something to my dad or Paul. Sometimes it was almost like having two dads.

"Well, I am just going to sit in the nursery and do my homework . . . if you don't mind." I could hear the snottiness in my voice as I tried to move past her.

"I don't mind at all, Beka . . . but you have to stop running sometime." She spoke quietly and looked directly in my eyes. I could feel the anger boiling inside, and I could only hope that my eyes reflected to her that I did not appreciate her comment. But I said nothing and headed directly for the nursery. She had no right to say anything to me. She didn't know anything about me. Who in the world did she think I was running from? I certainly hadn't gone anywhere. There was nowhere to go.

Before I even reached the nursery I heard the music and singing begin. That was actually my favorite part of youth group when I used to come. The music would play and I could kind of close my eyes and disappear. It was the only time I felt any peace. It never lasted very long. I never even sang the words because I never felt the words were true. I fought an urge to go up to the sanctuary and be a part of what they were doing. I couldn't. I couldn't admit that I needed them or anyone else. I was going to have to handle this mess on my own.

The ride home was as silent as the ride there, but it was even worse when we got home. As soon as she went through the back door, Lucy began telling Paul all about the message she heard that night and then repeated the whole thing when Dad came home. Even after hearing it twice, I still didn't understand what she was so excited about. She seemed to be so amazed, and Dad and Paul were so enthusiastic it made my stomach do flip-flops inside of me. More and more I felt like I was not a part of this family . . . like I had been dropped here from another planet. I couldn't connect. I excused myself as soon as I could and went to my room.

I couldn't help but notice the look Dad and Paul exchanged as I said good night. I crawled right into bed. Sleep seemed to be the only reasonable way to escape my own thoughts.

I shiver as I stand by the side of the road. How did I get here? I look to my right and see the car approaching slowly. It's blue. My mother's car. To my left I see the pickup truck. It's old and orange, and the black smoke from the tailpipe stains the air around it. I wave my arms at the pickup. Is the driver asleep? Why isn't he on the right side of the road? I look back at my mother's car still moving forward slowly. Frantic, I yell into the crisp, cold air, "Get out of the way! Get out of the way! You're going to hit her! Don't you see her?"

In slow motion, it happens. My mother's blue car turns towards the shoulder to miss the pickup truck. The rear tires skid on the ice and the truck hits the back end of the small car, sending it spinning down the road. Then slowly it spins towards the *embankment and disappears down the hill. I run to where the tire marks stopped. "Mom? Mom!" I can't see the car. I can't hear anything. "Mom?"*

* * *

As soon as I woke up, I knew it was not going to be a good day. I could hear the rain pounding on the roof above my head, and it took everything I had not to turn over and bury my head under my pillows. I couldn't go back to sleep at that point, but I didn't want to get up either. So I just lay there.

"Beka, are you still asleep?" I heard Lucy's voice as she knocked gently on the door. I glanced at the clock, amazed that I had slept that long. She knocked again.

"Come in!" I yelled. I took a deep breath and tried to think of something to say to her. I was still angry with her.

Lucy poked her head through the door as I sat up in my bed. "Dad asked me to come up and make sure you were getting up. No one had heard you up yet and we thought you maybe overslept." She looked uncomfortable as she hovered over the threshold.

"Well, I'm up. Anything else I can do for you?" I spit the words out of my mouth.

"No." She turned and reached for the door but then stopped. She slowly turned back around.

"Actually, yes. You can tell me what's wrong with you. Why are you so angry?"

"I don't suppose that's any of your business, now is it?"

"Well, I have to live in the same house, eat at the

same table, and use the same bathroom as you. I think I have a right to know what is wrong with you."

"You make it sound like I'm mentally ill or something." I threw the covers off and began to rummage through my drawers.

"I didn't say that; you did." Lucy was standing taller, unafraid of the confrontation.

"You just thought it." I walked past her to go to the bathroom.

"Beka, you don't know . . . Beka, would you at least listen?" Her voice followed me down the hall. I turned to look at her.

"Go away, Lucy. Just go away." I turned back around and slammed the bathroom door behind me. Without even raising my voice I had managed to be cruel. I slid down the door and sat on the cold linoleum. Lucy's question echoed in my head. *What is wrong with you?* I didn't know. I just didn't know.

I stayed upstairs until the last moment so that I could walk through the kitchen and straight out the back door. I didn't want to see anybody.

I made it all the way out to my car before Paul caught up with me. "Beka, what in the world do you think you're doing?" he asked loudly. He looked frustrated, which gave me some satisfaction.

"I'm going to school. What do you think I'm doing?" I said just as loudly. I slammed the car door and started the engine. Then Paul opened the car door and reached past me. Before I knew what had happened, he had turned the car off and was walking away with my keys.

"Give those back to me!" I screamed. He stopped and turned around and strode back to the car.

He leaned towards me and said no, very quietly.

"You are not my father, and you can't tell me what to do, Paul. You think you run my life, but you don't. You better back off," I said just as quietly. He looked at me for a moment and straightened up.

"Beka, you need to get a clue that this family cares about what happens to you. You can't just keep blowing us off and then expect us to come running when you want help." He dropped the keys on the ground and walked away.

"I didn't ask for anyone's help, and believe me, you won't ever hear me ask!" I yelled at his back.

*   *   *

Halfway to school, I remembered that I had forgotten to ask my dad about eating over at Lori's. I shrugged my shoulders. I had told him about it yesterday. He would probably remember. I put it out of my mind.

*   *   *

As I walked down the hallway towards my locker, I could hear everyone talking about *Annie*. It sounded like a lot of people were planning on trying out. My heart sank as I realized I probably didn't have much of a chance of getting a part. I chided myself for even getting my hopes up in the first place.

"Good morning, Beka." I turned around to see Lori standing behind me with a tentative smile on her face.

"Well, hello there." She seemed to relax as I returned the smile.

"I talked to Megan and David last night and they said tonight would be fine for you to come to dinner. You still up for it?"

"Sure," I said, "but how do you want to work it? I could follow you home or . . ."

"Oh, I don't have a car . . . Megan usually picks me up."

"Oh, well, you could ride with me and show me how to get to your house and all," I suggested.

"That'll probably be fine. Are you sure you don't mind?"

"Not at all," I reassured her.

"Super. Well, I'll call Megan after lunch and let her know . . . I'm really glad you're coming. Well, I'd better scoot. . . . See you in second." She disappeared down the hallway.

*   *   *

The day began rather uneventfully. Gretchen was absent again, so it was one less thing to worry about. At lunch, Lori and I barely got a chance to talk at all. We arranged to meet at my locker after the last bell, but as soon as she had finished eating, she took off to call Megan to make sure she could ride with me to her house. I sat by myself at the table and picked at the rest of my lunch. I thought about the play tryouts. After this morning, I felt more desperate than ever to get a part. I would be so busy with the play that maybe everyone would lay off me for a while. I kind of felt like I had become the black sheep of the family. I didn't even know how it had happened. All I knew is that I wanted to be as far away as possible.

In journalism we worked on publishing our December edition. Of course, the top story was the spring musical tryouts. There were to be two days of auditions, and callbacks would be on Monday of the following week. Our student editor, Jen Burk, wanted to wait until the following Wednesday to publish so that we could include the cast list. As we set the type, I kept staring at the big empty spot on the screen where the cast list would go. I had decided to audition on Thursday to get it over with. Gretchen had this big elaborate explanation as to why you should audition on Friday, but I knew I would get so nervous waiting that I'd probably leave before I even auditioned.

I thought it was odd that I was all wound up about this audition. I, who never did anything like this, was hanging an awful lot of hope on it. I felt just like a thin little Christmas tree branch trying to hold on to an ornament that was too heavy, yet I had to hang on because it was my only hope. Then maybe things at home would just smooth out, and I'd never have to explain myself or make anybody understand . . . I could go on, just as if nothing had ever happened.

CHAPTER 8

Becoming Beka   BECOMING BEKA

I could see Lori waiting at my locker as I rounded the corner to the front hall. I began to wonder if this dinner thing was such a good idea. I felt a small twinge of a feeling that I really should go find Paul and let him know where I was going. But I shrugged it off. He didn't have to know everything I was doing.

Lori was unusually quiet as we walked out to the car, but I figured she was just nervous. After all, I was pretty nervous myself. I started the car so it could get warmed up.

"Beka, I wanted to talk to you about my family before we actually get there," Lori said quietly without looking up.

"Sure," I told her. "It'll take the car a few minutes to get warmed up enough for the heat to come on anyway." I tried to think of a way to lighten the mood, but she looked so serious that I just sat quietly and waited for her to begin.

"Okay, well," she said and took a deep breath, "I suppose I should have told you before this but I didn't want anyone at school to know. Megan isn't really my mother, but I guess you've figured that out by now. She and David are my foster parents. I was placed with them a few weeks ago."

She looked at me for a response. I tried not to look as startled as I felt. I knew kids who had two parents, one parent, grandparents, and stepparents, even kids who lived with their mom's boyfriend or dad's girlfriend. I had never known anyone, at least personally, who was in foster care. But I did know that most kids were in foster care because they had been neglected or abused. I didn't know if I should ask any questions though. She had already told me more than other kids knew.

"Where are your parents?" I asked cautiously. "You don't have to tell me if you don't want to."

"No, it's okay. I guess that's part of the story too. My dad was killed in a motorcycle accident when I was eleven. We never had a lot of money when I was growing up, but when he died, it was like we lost everything. Mom had a hard time when he died. She stopped going to work, stopped cleaning the house, and started drinking. My teachers started asking questions, and I really tried to protect my mom. I lied to them and told them everything was fine. But it wasn't. Because she wouldn't work we had no money for food or clothes or anything. What we did have—well, she had her friends go buy her beer and stuff.

"I guess the neighbors or my teachers or somebody called Child Protective Services, and somebody came out to our house. Well, you can just imagine what they found. My mom was passed out on the couch, the house was a wreck, and there was no food in the kitchen. Besides that, our electricity had been turned off the week before because Mom wasn't paying the bills. They took me away with them that day. My mom never even woke up when I kissed her good-bye."

Tears trickled down her face, and she wiped them away as quickly as they fell. I fumbled in my purse for some tissues and handed her the package.

"Social services sent me to live with Michelle and Michael O'Grady. They had two of their own children, Stephen and Melissa, and one other foster child, Ellen, living with them. It wasn't a bad place at all. They were all very nice. It was kind of strange after being an only child to be one of four, but it was nice to have people around. They told me it would only be until my mom got herself straightened out. My caseworker, Liz Green, arranged for me to visit with my mom once a week at the social services building. Every week Liz would pick me up, and every week my mom didn't show up. About two months after I was put in foster care, the police got a call from our old neighbors. The police went to the house and found my mother dead from a drug overdose."

"Wow, Lori, I'm so sorry. I had no idea." I shook my head, at a loss for anything else to say.

"I stayed with the O'Gradys up until two weeks ago. You see, the O'Gradys decided to move to Ohio to take a job offer at a plant out there. But I couldn't go with them unless they adopted me. They decided they didn't want to, so Liz placed me with the Rollinses. She told me that's it's rare that a kid my age gets adopted. I could be in foster care until I'm eighteen."

She paused for a moment and began to smile. "It's funny though. Life has a way of turning out for the best. The O'Gradys never talked about adopting me, not in the whole five years I lived with them, but David and Megan have been talking about it since the day I walked in their door . . . and they barely know me at all! It may be too much to hope for, but it can't hurt, I guess. You know, Beka, I'm glad I told you. It helps to know that someone else knows."

I pulled out of the parking lot with my mind racing. It's strange how when you hear about someone else's problems, yours seem pretty insignificant, yet I couldn't shake the thought that I could never share my secret like Lori had shared hers. After all, it wasn't Lori who had done anything wrong, like I had. She wasn't to blame for what happened. I knew that I was definitely to blame for my predicament. I wondered what she would think of me if she knew my secret.

Lori guided me to her house, and she was fairly bouncing with excitement by the time we pulled in the driveway. The front door swung open as a small girl with long red hair bounded down the front stairs. For a moment, I thought it was Anna coming out to greet me. A few moments later, a woman came out after the small child.

"Kari Lynn, please come back in this house. It is way too cold for you to be out here without your coat." The woman took the girl's hand and walked her back inside the house and closed the door. The woman waited on the front porch for us. The child pressed her face against the front window and kept waving and yelling, "Hi, Lori! Lori's home!"

As we got out of the car, the woman smiled and said, "You must be the Rebekah we've been hearing about. It's wonderful to meet you!"

She turned her attention to Lori as we came up the stairs. Lori ran up on the porch and hugged her. "You were right!" she said breathlessly. "I feel so much better. I told her everything before we came over!"

"I'm glad," she said with a smile. "Come in, Rebekah. I'm sure Kari Lynn is dying to meet you!"

After the introductions, Lori and I went up to her room. It was nicely decorated with soft greens and blues. She didn't have a lot of things in her room, just the basics. There was a picture frame on her nightstand. When she saw me looking at it, she walked over and picked it up. "It's my mom and dad," she said as she handed me the frame. The picture was of a young-looking couple holding hands on a beach. The wind must have been blowing that day. They looked very happy. It was eerie to think that both of those happy looking people were dead. I sighed thinking about the pictures of my mother in my own house. It seemed selfish to complain about it, though, with someone who lost everyone in her world.

"So," Lori said with a yawn. "What shall we do until dinner?"

"I don't know . . . it's your house. What do you want to do?"

"Tell me about your family. I know you have two sisters and one brother, but you didn't tell me much about them. And you haven't told me anything about your parents. It must be so much fun to be in a full house like that." She smiled and hugged her knees to her chest. She looked expectantly at me. I had forgotten that Lori wouldn't know about my mom. I never had to tell anyone about it before. When your mother's death makes the front page of the local newspaper, you really don't need to let anyone know. But Lori was new here, and apparently the whispers about me must have tapered off at school more than I had realized.

"Well, there's not much to tell. They're just normal brothers and sisters. Actually, Kari Lynn could be Anna's twin. I thought it was her when she came out the door. No one has said anything to you about my mom?" I asked her.

"No," she shrugged. "Why should they? I haven't really met that many people. Why?"

"Well, my mother was killed in a car accident earlier this year."

Lori's eyes opened like saucers. "Really?"

"Yeah."

"Do you want to tell me about it? You don't have to if you don't want to."

"There really isn't much to tell. She was a doctor. A pediatrician actually. She had to go to the hospital late one night because of a little boy who had suddenly gotten very sick. There had been an ice storm the day before, and she and my dad figured the roads were clear enough for her to go alone. He had driven her in the truck the day before. So she left to go to the hospital. She called about an hour later to say that she was on her way home, but she never made it. An oncoming car lost control and they collided. Both cars ended up off the road. The rescue people told us she was killed instantly. 'A freak accident' they called it. Wrong place, wrong time."

"When did it happen?"

"March 12 of this year."

"Wow, you seem to be doing really well. I couldn't have told you about my mom like that if it had happened that recently. I've had five years to deal with my mom's death. You must be strong."

"Not really," I told her. "You had twice as much to deal with, Lori. I don't know what I would have done if my dad had been in that car with her. I don't know if I could have handled it if I'd lost them both."

"Sure you would have. I handle it because I have to. We're never given a choice about the cards we're dealt. We just have to cope. That's really all I've done." She paused for a moment. "So this will be your first Christmas without her?"

I just nodded. The lump in my throat prevented me from speaking.

"You know, when my mom died, it took me a couple of months to really accept the idea that she was even gone. Liz would talk to me about it all the time. She said that some people don't get over the shock of it for a long time, and once they do, they need to have time to grieve. But you can't grieve when you're in shock. She said it could take a few years to really get through it. You're doing fine. Even if it doesn't feel like you are."

I looked at her and wondered if I should tell her more. Tell her about how I'm not handling it very well. That I wasn't doing okay. That she was practically the only person I have ever spoken with about my mom's death. But the words wouldn't come. I couldn't say anything. It was like those nightmares where you can't scream for help though you try and try.

A knock at the door startled us both out of the silence.

"I wanted to let you two know that dinner will be ready in just a few minutes. Oh, and Rebekah, does your father have our phone number here? I'd like him to be able to reach you if he needs to."

"Umm, no, I don't think so."

"Would you call home before dinner and give them the number?" She smiled and closed the door softly after I told her I would.

"You can use the phone up here." Lori stood up and pulled the phone over to where we were sitting. "You can read the number to him off of the phone."

I hesitated. I knew I had mentioned this dinner to my dad the day before, but I didn't know if he would remember. I looked at my watch and realized my dad was probably just getting home. I dialed the number slowly, hoping that Anna would answer.

"Hello!" came the cheerful voice of my youngest sister. I breathed a heavy sigh of relief.

"Hey, sweetie! It's Beka."

"Beka! Everyone's been calling everywhere looking

for you! Where are you? Are you comin' home? I'll go get Paul and tell him it's you."

"No, Anna, wait a minute, just tell him—" I heard the phone drop onto the counter and Anna's voice yelling Paul's name in the distance. Just what I needed. I considered hanging up, but Lori was sitting there looking at me. She knew I hadn't given out the number yet. I decided to get it over with as quickly as possible.

"Beka!" Paul said sharply as he picked up the phone.

"I don't know why you all are freaking out over nothing. I told Dad yesterday that I was going to eat over at a friend's house. I was just calling to—"

"'Told' or 'asked,' Beka? Because you never confirmed with anybody this morning that you weren't going to be here."

I ignored his question and continued. "I only called to give you the number where I am at. It's 555-4987. I'm going to have dinner over here and I'll be home before nine o'clock. Good-bye." I hung up the phone carefully. I had tried to keep my tone pleasant because Lori was still sitting across from me. I smiled at her and said, "All taken care of."

"Everything okay?" Lori looked concerned as she moved the phone back to the desk.

I shrugged, "Just some family drama. No big deal."

"Family drama, huh?" She smiled. "I know all about family drama."

"You never said much about the other family you lived with, the O . . ."

"O'Gradys. Yeah, well, there's not a lot to tell. With the three other kids in the house I was kind of wallpaper

75

there. They were nice enough and all, but I never felt like I really fit there."

"Was it scary, though? When they decided to move without you?"

"At first, yes," Lori said as she grabbed a pillow off the bed and laid down on her belly. "I never really clicked with the O'Gradys, but it was safe there, and I had no idea where I could end up. I knew Liz would do her best but . . . I was still scared. When you are in the system you are at the mercy of the system. Liz has always been a lifeline for me. She's the one that really kept me . . . well, gave me perspective, I guess."

"So, you're happy here?" It seemed like the right thing to ask even though I knew the answer.

"Happy doesn't describe it. It's just so different. From the moment we met they were interested in me, wanted to know about me. I've gotten more attention in the last two weeks than I have in years. It's nice—I hope it's still nice two months from now; I am sort of used to being left to my own. I have a feeling the rules are going to be a lot tighter. But honestly, I just feel *right* here. C'mon, then, let's go downstairs and see if we can help with anything." Lori jumped up and held out her hand to help me up. I took it and she pulled me to my feet and laughed. "I just know we are going to be great friends!"

I followed her down the stairs, wondering how long all this was going to last.

*   *   *

"So, you're one of the Madison kids, right?" Megan asked as we were setting the table.

"Yes, ma'am." I wondered how much she knew about my family.

"Your mom was Kari Lynn's doctor. She was a really wonderful woman. I was very sorry to hear about the accident."

"Thank you." I looked up only briefly. It was hard to hear someone say how wonderful she was. Because it was true. She was wonderful and she deserved better than what she got from me. I bit my lip to keep the tears from welling up. Suddenly I felt Megan's arm go around my shoulder. She was so close I could smell her perfume. I closed my eyes and imagined it was my mother's arm. The tears began to escape from my eyes, and I quickly excused myself to use the rest room. I needed to gain my composure. I closed the door and washed my face. I was so frustrated with myself. I just couldn't seem to keep my cool lately. I had gone for months without being emotional after she died. Lately, I couldn't get through a day without fighting the tears. I was going to have to work harder, be more careful.

I was content to just listen as the Rollinses chatted away. Megan seemed to be able to include me without asking me to participate. She'd smile and make eye contact. I just felt relaxed, like there was no pressure. I could see why Lori had taken to her so quickly. She didn't really act like a grown-up. Some grown-ups get strange when they talk to teenagers, like that Susan Matthews at church—they get all condescending. But Megan just seemed interested, like she really cared.

"Did I tell you that Megan's a photographer?" Lori asked me just as we were finishing up.

"Really?" That touched a nerve. I had never really talked to anybody about my interest in photography before. All I did was take pictures for the yearbook and *The Bragg About*, but I had never met a real photographer.

"Do you like photography, Beka?" Megan ventured.

I nodded but I didn't want to seem too eager. "Yeah, well, I take pictures for school, but I don't know that much about it."

"Megan has her own studio. You should come see it sometime." Lori began clearing the dishes, so I jumped up to help as well.

"Yes, you're welcome anytime. And I'd love to see your work sometime," Megan added.

*   *   *

I left soon after dinner was over, explaining that I needed to get my homework done. Megan hugged me as I left, telling me to come over anytime. There was something so comforting about her, but she had eyes like Paul's. It was like she could also see right through me. I had never considered my pictures to be "my work" before. The thought satisfied me somewhere inside. Maybe there was more to me than I thought.

I pulled into my driveway wondering what awaited me on the inside. My dad was in the kitchen as I walked in the back door.

"I would like to talk with you before you go upstairs,

Beka." His tone was quiet but firm. I knew that he was not happy with me.

"Sure, what?" I said lightly, trying to show him I was not concerned. I hadn't really done anything wrong anyway, except not reminding someone this morning.

"Let's sit down." He gestured towards the kitchen table. I was still holding my backpack, car keys, and jacket, so I sat down with everything on my lap. It made me feel less vulnerable.

"I'd like to know why you did what you did tonight." He folded his hands and leaned forward on the table. He looked right at me and waited. I hated it when he made me talk first.

"I'm not sure what I did, except go to a friend's house for dinner. I've always been allowed to do that, haven't I?" I tried to not sound angry, but I could feel myself growing defensive.

"Yes, as long as we know where you are. I know that you mentioned going to a friend's house in passing last night, but you never checked with me to make sure that was all right or give me this person's name or phone number."

"And I called with all that information earlier," I reminded him.

"Does that make up for not doing things properly to begin with?"

"I don't know. I didn't think it was such a big deal. Why are we making a big production out of this?"

"Because of your track record lately. You haven't been communicating with anybody. You seem upset and angry. You have not been treating your family with much respect. I want to make sure you don't begin making poor decisions or start breaking the rules of this house. I love you, and those rules are there for a purpose."

He waited for me to respond, but I just sat there, his words still stinging in my ears.

"Well, Beka. What do you think we should do about this?"

I sat completely still.

"Beka, I asked you a question. I'd like you to answer me."

I shrugged my shoulders. He sighed with exasperation.

"Fine. Then your consequence for not seeking approval before you went out and for not informing anyone of your whereabouts until after you were already there will be as follows. You will lose your car privileges for two weeks, and there will be no outings this weekend. I hope you will remember that you need to ask before you do something. I worry about you when I don't know where you are." He stood up and knelt by my chair. "I love you, Beka, and I hope you will come and talk with me about why you handled this situation this way. I don't want it to happen in the future."

He reached out his arms to hug me, but I stood up and walked past him to leave. I turned to drop my car keys on the table. "I made a commitment to do something after school on Thursday and Monday. May I have your permission to stay after school those days?" I spoke towards the floor. I couldn't even look at him.

"What did you make a commitment to do?" he asked as he stood up.

"Never mind. Forget it—it's not important." I turned to leave, feeling deflated. Now I wouldn't even be able to try out for the play.

"Beka, wait. I don't mind if you stay after school. I appreciate you asking me. I just would like to know what you are doing." He added quietly, "I'd like to know what's going on in your life, sweetheart."

I stopped. I didn't know what to do. I didn't want anyone to know I was trying out for this play, because if I failed, I wanted to fail alone. I didn't want anyone feeling sorry for me if I didn't make it. But I also wanted to try.

"It's just some silly play at school that a bunch of the girls are auditioning for. I promised them I would be there." I tried to make it sound like it wasn't that important to me.

"Oh, all right. Will you be auditioning as well?"

"I don't know yet."

"Well, that's fine. Paul can come pick you up when you are finished at school. You'll just need to call him. Okay?"

I nodded and went upstairs. I waited until I got to my room. Then I curled up on my bed and cried. I wanted to disappear.

I decided to skip breakfast and avoid the family thing the next morning. I went downstairs just as everybody was leaving. The ride to school was very quiet. Paul didn't even say anything to me until we turned into the senior parking lot.

"Do you know what time you'll be finished this afternoon? Dad told me you needed to stay."

"I don't know," I said with a shrug. "I can just get a ride home with someone."

"No, Dad said I was to come get you. I'll swing by around five. If you need to get home before that, just call." With that he slammed the car door and walked towards the building. I got out of the car slowly. It made me so uncomfortable when Paul was upset with me. It was so much easier when I was the one upset with him.

*   *   *

By the time lunchtime rolled around, I wasn't sure I was going to go through with the audition. I was nervous, and I had already overheard five different conversations about who was going to get which part. I probably didn't even have a chance. Gretchen was back in school, and she kept passing notes to me during second period about the play and the latest gossip. She kept writing that I had a good chance and that it was going to be *so* much fun.

At lunch, Lori chattered about how much Megan and David and Kari Lynn liked me and how she couldn't wait to meet my family. I didn't have the heart to tell her that I wasn't going to be inviting anyone to my house anytime in the near future.

"Isn't your audition today?" she asked as we were leaving the cafeteria.

"Yeah, but I'm not so sure I want to do it anymore."

"Why not?"

"Well, I get the feeling that the whole thing has already been cast. I don't think I have much of a chance."

"Oh, people are just talking. You never know who they're going to cast. And didn't you say you've never tried out for one of these things before? Well, then nobody knows how good you are yet. You'll just have to show them in the audition what you can do and then don't worry about it. The worst that can happen is that you don't get a part, right? And you definitely won't get one if you don't try, so what do you have to lose?"

I laughed. "You know, Lori, I do believe you should be a lawyer. You have very convincing arguments." She was also one of the nicest people I had ever known. Her encouragement kept me afloat.

"Well, we better get to class. Good luck! And call me tonight to tell me how it went." She waved as she went down the hallway, and I turned to go into my chemistry class.

By the time the final bell rang, I was still nervous but determined to at least try. I went to my locker to get my homework and coat and headed for the auditorium. There were a lot of people there. I worked my way towards the stage door where people were signing up for time slots. I looked at the list and found that someone had already written my name into the third slot. I went to go find Gretchen.

I went into the band practice room and found her sitting on the floor with Mai, Chrissy, Theresa, and Lizzy. When she saw me she waved me over to come sit with them on the floor. I dropped my backpack and coat on the ground and sat down.

"I already signed you up. I got you the earliest slot I could. If you are determined to go on the first day, you have to go early, before they see too many people."

"But third?"

"It'll be fine. You want them to see you before they get too tired of listening."

"Then why don't you go today too?"

"Because they're going to decide about callbacks

tomorrow after everybody goes. That way I'll be fresh in their mind." She smiled and tossed her hair and giggled. The other girls giggled too.

"When are you all going?" I asked. I wasn't too sure yet about how they felt about me being around.

"I'm going right after you," Theresa spoke up. "And Chrissy is going after me. Mai, Lizzy, and Gretchen are going tomorrow."

"Then why is everybody here today?" I asked.

"To be supportive," Gretchen said as she handed me a bottle of lemon juice. "And to check out the competition. Here, drink some of this. It will help clear your throat out."

*　　　*　　　*

Before long they called the first person to go onto the stage. Because we were going so early, we went and sat in the hallway by the stage door so we would hear our names. We had already done some voice warm-ups, led by Gretchen of course, so there was nothing to do but sit and wait. And get nervous.

When my name was called, Gretchen and I both stood up.

"Bruce already has your music in there, so don't worry. Break a leg!" The other girls waved as I was ushered through the door by Michael Goodall. He was the student director for the production.

"Okay, what you're going to do is walk out to where the spotlight is shining in the center of the stage. The directors will ask for your name and height and then you will sing your song. Wait for them to dismiss you before you leave. Break a leg!"

I walked out onto the dark stage towards the light that was shining in the center. When I reached the spot I stood quietly. I was sure they could hear my heart pounding in my chest. I heard a voice from the blackness in front of me. "Please state your full name and your height."

"Rebekah Madison. I'm five foot two."

"Thank you. You may sing your selection."

Bruce began to play the music, and at first I wasn't sure that I was going to be able to make anything come out of my throat. The first part of the song is talking, and after a few moments, it just happened. About halfway through the song I remembered the movements I was supposed to be doing. I just kind of lost myself. It was an incredible feeling. It was like I really was this person. I could feel her sorrow and frustration. Before I knew it, I was singing the last line.

"Thank you, Rebekah. I have one more request. Would you pick up the script on the stage and read the highlighted section on page 45? I would like you to speak as loudly as you can without yelling."

I picked up the script and fumbled for page 45. Gretchen had not mentioned anything about reading from the script. All the confidence I had gained during the singing quickly drained out of me. It was Molly's lines that were highlighted in the script. Someone in the audience read the other character's lines.

"Thank you very much."

Michael appeared at my side and led me back to the stage door. It took a few moments to allow my eyes to adjust to the bright hallway. Michael called Theresa's name, and they disappeared through the stage door.

"How'd it go? What happened? Did they say anything?" The questions all came at once.

"I'm not sure," I shrugged. "I guess it went okay. I had to read some lines from the script. I wasn't expecting that."

"Really?" Gretchen seemed genuinely surprised. "I wonder why. I've done this for two years and I've never read from the script."

"It's probably because they don't know me. I've never tried out for these things before."

"You know, you're probably right," she said quickly. She seemed relieved. I knew that she wanted to be Annie. Gretchen always wanted the lead in everything. She had played just small roles in the last two productions. Maybe she was nervous. She hadn't really seen me as competition before. I wasn't sure that I was anyway. But there was a little part of me that was pretty excited. Maybe it meant that I was really being considered for something other than the chorus.

Since I had gone so early, I stayed until just before five with the others and then went out to meet my brother. Gretchen seemed disappointed that I wasn't going to be able to hang out with them during the auditions the next day, but I told her I couldn't help it. I was disappointed to hear that callbacks wouldn't be posted until Monday morning. It was going to be a long weekend of waiting.

Paul pulled up just as I was coming out of the building. I climbed into the car hoping that he wouldn't ask me about what I was doing. So much for hoping.

"So did you audition for the play?" he asked quietly.

I nodded but didn't say anything.

"That's great!" he said as he grinned. "I think that sounds pretty cool. Though I must admit that I was pretty surprised when Dad told me why you needed a ride home. You never were interested in that kind of stuff before, were you?"

"I never tried it before, so how could I know if I was interested or not?" I couldn't get the irritation out of my voice. I knew that Paul was trying to make up with me, but I just couldn't seem to relax and allow myself to forgive him. It was too dangerous. If I relaxed and opened up to him again, I wouldn't be able to take it back. He would see too much of what was going on inside. No, it was safer to be distant. He wouldn't understand anyway.

*　　*　　*

The kitchen was buzzing with laughter as we came through the door. The CD player had been turned on and Lucy was dancing around with Anna to the strains of DC Talk's "In the Light." Mary was laughing and handing plates and cups and silverware to anyone who passed by her. They would take them and dance to the table. Paul washed his hands and started making the salad for dinner.

"Beka, Beka, Beka!" Anna yelled when she saw me in the doorway. She came and threw her arms around me. "Come and dance with me!"

"Not now, sweetie. I'm going to go upstairs. You go ahead, okay?" I tried to say it as nicely as possible. I just wasn't in the mood for all this merriment. I needed to get away.

"Are you still feeling bad? Daddy said we gotta give you time because you're feeling bad. I been waitin' and waitin'. Are you ever going to feel good?" She looked up at me with her big blue eyes, but I couldn't think of anything to say to her. So I smoothed her red hair, kissed her on the forehead, and left her standing there.

Lucy had been watching from the table, and when I looked back, she had walked over to Anna and scooped her up and was spinning her around. I couldn't tell what she was saying to her. But I guessed that it couldn't be any worse than what she had already been told. I got angrier as I walked up the stairs. I wanted to know what my dad and Paul were saying to all of them. I felt like such an outcast. I didn't belong here anymore. I guess I never did. I had been fooling myself to think that everything would just cool off. It had turned into this big crisis, and I wasn't sure it was going to go away without me having to talk to them. I didn't want to be forced into confessing. I couldn't confess. They would never trust me again. I was sure of it.

I reluctantly came back downstairs for dinner. They were just getting ready to sit down, so I quietly took my place. Dad prayed over the meal and then looked up at me expectantly.

"So, tell us about this play, Beka. How did your audition go?" he asked. Four pairs of eyes looked at me, waiting for me to respond. I didn't know what to say. I didn't want this to happen; I didn't want anybody to know. I could feel my nose and eyes stinging. Why did they have

to ruin it? Now there was going to be all this expectation. I didn't want them feeling sorry or happy for me
when the results were posted. I wanted to do it alone.

I shrugged and mumbled, "I don't know." I hoped
that they would just drop it.

"Well, what play is it? What's it about?" my dad asked
as he continued passing food around the table. I just sat
there awkwardly. I couldn't speak. I knew I couldn't talk
without my voice cracking. The silence was deafening.

"It's *Annie*, Dad." Paul spoke up, obviously seeing that
I wasn't going to answer. I just stared at the food on my
plate.

"It's about an orphan named Annie. She thinks her
parents are coming back for her, and she meets a rich
man that helps her look for them," Lucy piped up after
another awkward silence.

"Oh," Dad said quietly. "Well, you have a beautiful
voice, Beka. I'm sure your audition went well. Is there a
particular part that you'd like to have?"

"Can I come see your play, Beka?" Anna asked.

I didn't know what to do. Everybody just kept looking at me.

"Just leave me alone about it," I finally blurted out.
Everyone got really still. I pushed my chair back from the
table and ran upstairs. I didn't even wait on the landing
to find out what they said after I left. I collapsed on my
bed and screamed into my pillow.

Fifteen minutes later, I had finally calmed down. I
felt really stupid. It would have been so much easier to
answer their questions. Now things would be twice as
awkward as they were before. What was I going to do?

I leaned over and picked up the phone. I had to call Lori like I had promised. Besides, maybe it would get my mind off of everything.

"Hello," a soft voice answered.

"Yes, may I please speak with Lori?"

"Oh, I'm sorry, she's out with her father right now. May I take a message?"

"No, that's okay—" I started to say.

"Beka, is that you? This is Megan. It was very nice to have you over last night. Kari Lynn cannot stop talking about it. I really appreciate your kindness towards Lori. I can't imagine how difficult it must be for her at times. How are you doing?"

Never in my life had an adult started talking with me like that. I had no idea what to do. I figured I could just be polite and get off the phone. "I'm fine, Mrs. Rollins. Thank you for having me over. Dinner was really good. You can just tell Lori I called."

"Please, go ahead and call me Megan."

"Uh, okay, uh, Megan. Well, I better go and um . . ."

"Oh, sure, of course. I'll tell Lori you called. You take care, Beka, and let me know if you ever need anything. Bye."

"Bye." I hung up the phone quickly. Even though the whole thing made me uncomfortable, I couldn't help marveling at how nice she was. She spoke to me like I was a real person. Kind of like my mom used to. I decided that since I couldn't go back downstairs that I should just do my homework and go to bed.

Tomorrow would be here too soon.

The truck hits *a bump and I slide*
along a rough, broken car seat. I can barely see through the wind-
shield. The man next to me grips the steering wheel tightly but his
eyes are half closed. I squint when the headlights flash in front of
me, and I turn to see if the man will move. His head has rolled
backward and his eyes are completely closed.

"Wake up! Wake up!" I yell at him. He doesn't move. He
doesn't even flinch.

"You're going to hit her. Please! Wake up!"

*　　*　　*

No one said a word to me the next morning. Even Anna, though she kept glancing at me out of the corner of her eye, never said a thing. I would rather have them all yell and scream at me. I wondered what Dad had said to them. Paul drove me silently to school. By the time we got there, I could feel the stinging in my nose and eyes. I know I probably hurt them last night, but I felt trapped. Were they all trying to get me back? Even as I thought it, I knew that they just probably didn't know what to say to me either. Knowing that didn't help me one bit though. I hurt. Everything hurt.

I tried to just slide through the day, but between Gretchen and Lori, I felt like I got some good practice at acting. I had to play cool and pretend like everything was just great. Gretchen slipped me notes all day. All about the play, of course, and mostly rumors. Because nobody knew anything. Lori was all excited about going with her family to their grandparents' house over the weekend. She must have said how excited she was about meeting her grandmother and grandfather a hundred times. Then she'd stop and say, "Oh, I said that already, didn't I? I'm just so excited!" I really was happy for her, but I was also confused. I mean, they weren't really her grandparents; the Rollinses weren't even her real family. She acted like the adoption was a done deal, but she had said that they had only talked about it. I wondered if something had happened that she hadn't told me about.

Then, on the way home, Paul decided to say something.

"You know, I've been thinking about this and praying about this all day. I don't know how to help you. I need to ask you to forgive me for being angry with you. Being angry isn't going to solve anything. Will you forgive me?" He paused, waiting for an answer. I hated it when he did that. Like I could say no even if I wanted to. So I just shrugged. I guess he took that as an answer, because he continued talking.

"How can I help you? How can we as a family help you?" He paused again. I kept staring and pulling at the gloves on my hands. I didn't know what to say. I tried waiting again, but he didn't say anything else. He just waited. I could see him glancing over at me every so often.

"Who says I need any help?" I said quietly.

"It doesn't take a genius to see that something is terribly wrong. Not talking about it isn't going to make it go away."

"Who says anything is wrong? Aren't I allowed to have a lousy day once in a while?"

"A day is one thing; weeks upon weeks is another." He stopped for a moment then continued. "Is it Christmas? Are you upset about the holidays coming and Mom not being here?"

"No, and even if I was, what are you supposed to do about it? Nobody can do anything to change the fact that she won't be here, so why are you asking me all these questions? I just want to be left alone." I turned as far as I could away from him.

He took the hint and didn't say anything else. But, as usual, my mind was racing. Part of me felt good that he loved me and was concerned about me. But the other part of me was still angry. I felt like I was being pushed and poked and prodded at and I just wanted it all to stop. I wished I could snap my fingers and rewind my life. Figure out where everything went sour and fix it. It wasn't even just the big lie anymore. It was more complicated than that. I thought back to Paul's question about what he could do. The thing that scared me the most was that I really didn't know. I didn't know what anybody could do to help me out of the pit I had crawled into. I used to think that if I just told them the truth about the "saved" thing that it would all be okay. But I didn't believe that would help anyway. Not anymore.

*　　*　　*

When we got home, Mary was still cooking dinner, and only Lucy had gotten home from school. I went straight to my room. It had become a sanctuary to me. A safe escape from the world. Since it was Friday, I dropped my book bag in a corner and decided to not even look at my homework until Sunday. I took a look at my caterpillars and was surprised to see one brand-new chrysalis hanging from a branch. Two of the caterpillars were still crawling along the bottom while the last one was hanging from another branch with his head curled up, getting ready to form the casing that would turn him into a butterfly. As I inspected the new chrysalis, the hanging caterpillar began to twist and writhe. I watched him as his small body pushed and pulled against itself, as if it was fighting the change that was about to take place. I thought he might die if he didn't stop. I shushed and cooed at the small caterpillar, trying to get him to stop twisting, to stop fighting. If he fell off the branch, he would never make it. I knew my words were useless, but I simply had to try.

"It's okay, little guy. It's supposed to happen. You just gotta let go and let it happen." For the first time I wondered if it hurt the caterpillars when their bodies turned into the chrysalis. I had never seen one fight the process like this one was. Maybe there was pain involved. Maybe I had simply missed the other ones when they became afraid. Even though I had always loved butterflies, perhaps prompted by the nickname my parents had always used for me, I had only begun raising them two years ago. I did it as a project for my freshman biology class and then just kept doing it. There was something so natural and amazing about watching a little caterpillar turn into a butterfly. During the spring and summer, I let them go into my mother's garden, but in the winter, they fluttered around in their netting drinking sugar water I mixed each day and sprinkled on carnations.

I pulled a pillow off my bed and lay on the floor by the bottom of the net, whispering softly to the writhing caterpillar. When he did finally stop twisting, I watched him carefully to see if he was all right. I couldn't tell. I would just have to wait and see.

I must have drifted off, because the next thing I knew, I felt the headphones being pulled off my ears. I looked up to see Lucy standing over me. She smiled.

"I came up to get you for dinner. Everything's ready and I wanted to warn you that we have company."

"Who?" I said as I rubbed my eyes and walked over to the dresser.

"Her name is Gabby Falcon. She works with Dad at the bank. She seems really nice. She's been here for about half an hour or so."

"I'll be down in a few minutes," I said quietly. I didn't want Lucy to think that just because we had a conversation, everything was peachy keen with us. She must have noticed the coldness in my tone because she kind of shrugged and said, "Okay," and headed out the door.

I took my time brushing my hair. What was Dad doing bringing a woman home? The longer I thought about it, the angrier I got. Mom died only nine months ago. How could he do this?

I trudged downstairs. Even before I went into the family room, I could hear laughter. I took a deep breath and rounded the corner. And there she was. Sitting on the sofa between Anna and Lucy. They all looked up as I came into the room. Dad stood and came over to me. He put his arm around my shoulder.

"Gabby, I'd like you to meet my second oldest, Beka. She's a junior and she's really smart. She'll probably get in anywhere she wants to go." Dad was beaming. He walked me over and sat me down on the last available chair, a hard wooden stool in the corner by the piano.

"So, Beka, did you get that driver's license yet?" Gabby turned to ask me. She was just smiling way too much.

"Yes, I did," I said politely. I didn't elaborate.

"Good for you," she said. "I had to wait till almost my senior year to get my license. I was the last person in my class to get it. I had a hard time waiting!" She looked at me to see if I was going to respond. When I didn't, she turned back to Anna on the couch. "I guess you have a while to wait too."

"I'm only eight," she giggled.

With that everybody laughed, except me. When Dad caught my eye though, I gave a quick smile. I could tell he was annoyed with me. I was glad he knew I wasn't happy. The conversation continued for a bit longer, without any involvement from me. Whenever Dad looked at me, I'd smile briefly, then continue being a bump on the stool.

Dinner was more of the same. Lots of laughter and questions. Gabby didn't try asking me any more questions. I asked to be excused as soon as I could find a break in the conversation.

"Why don't you join us? I think the girls want to play a game of Pictionary or something."

"No, thank you," I said curtly. "I have some things I want to do tonight."

"Well, all right then. Come back down later, though, if you want."

I cleared my plate and went back to my room. As I walked up the stairs I could hear my phone ringing. I ran to get it.

"Hello?" I said, quite out of breath.

"Finally!" Gretchen said loudly. "I've been trying to call you for the last hour. Do you have something against voice mail?"

"Hello to you too, Gretch," I said as I flopped onto the bed.

"Well, you won't believe what happened at the auditions today!"

"What? What?" I said quickly. I was genuinely interested in chatting with Gretchen. How bizarre! A week
ago I avoided her like the plague, and now she was calling me.

"Well," Gretchen said dramatically, "you know Anne
Blankenship and Laura Steele, right?"

"Of course, don't they usually have the leads in these
things?"

"Exactly!" Gretchen said excitedly. "Only Anne
decided not to try out this year! Can you believe it?"

"No way. Why would she drop out her senior year?"

"Something about trying for bigger and better things
than a high school musical. Supposedly she has some
audition for a regional theater in the city."

"That is pretty exciting."

"No, that's not what's exciting! It's her not trying out
that's exciting. That means that Laura is my, I mean, our
only competition. She'll probably get Miss Hannigan,
leaving Annie open for *moi!*" I could practically hear her
tossing her hair over the telephone.

"Wow, so your audition went well?"

"Of course it did. I am so excited. Anyhow, my party
mood cannot sit here in this boring house tonight. We're
having a soiree over at Mai's house. Her parents are out
of town so we'll start around ten, okay? Do you know
where her house is?"

"Oh, well, I . . . I mean, I can't go."

"What? Why not? This is my big break. Well, not the
big one, but an important one. You can't let me down."

"I'm grounded . . . and I lost my car privileges."

"What did you do, rob a bank?"

"No, it's dumb. I didn't tell my dad about something."

"Wow, what a jerk!"

"No, I knew better." I didn't like her saying that about my dad.

"Well," she said slowly, "you can sneak out and I can come and pick you up. But you have to be ready by ten of, so that we can get there in time to help Mai set up."

"I don't know, Gretch. What if I get caught?"

"Here comes Beka the Prude again. Get over it Bek; live a little! I'll wait at the corner of Broad and Picker Street. That's not too far for you to walk. I'll be there at 9:50. Don't be late!" With that, she hung up the phone. I stared at the phone for what seemed like forever. What was I going to do?

I really didn't have a choice. I had to go. Gretchen would never forgive me if I didn't go. It felt too good to have friends again to blow it. I had never snuck out of the house before, though. I had to make sure I covered my tracks. As I crept down the stairs and down the hall towards the family room, I could hear them shouting out words. I assumed they were playing a game. Gabby and my dad must have been sitting by the door, because I could hear them talking as the game was going on.

"It's only been the last few months that it's been like this, really. But it's getting worse. I'm not sure what to do," my dad said.

"Well, is it something that you can just keep an eye on? Maybe she just needs time," Gabby offered.

"Maybe you're right. I'm just worried that—"

I chose that moment to step into the room. My dad's words halted abruptly, and they both looked up at me from the couch. I was thrilled that Dad looked as though he felt awkward. He had no right to talk about me to a total stranger.

"I just wanted to let you know that I have a bad headache. I'm going to bed. It was nice meeting you, Gabby. Good night." I was trying not to grit my teeth while I said it, but I wasn't sure I did very well.

My dad jumped up off the couch. "Wait, honey." He put his arm around my shoulder. "Is there anything I can do?"

"I already took some Tylenol. I just want to go to bed. I'm sure I'll feel better in the morning. Good night." I walked out of the room and up the stairs. I was positive that Dad would never know I was gone. I glanced at my watch. I had nearly an hour before I had to meet Gretchen. I got ready slowly, working up my anticipation of the party. I put on some music, very softly. I thought about Gretchen and everything that had happened this week. It was so strange to think that someone actually wanted me at a party. I was really nervous because I had never been to one. I wondered if Mark was going to be there.

With everything that had been happening over the last year, I never bothered to think about boys much. They never seemed to think about me much either. But before Mom died, I had noticed Mark. His one major flaw was that he hung out with Jeremy, Lance, and some of the other more popular boys sometimes. Jeremy and Gretchen were an on-again, off-again couple, and Lance was seeing Mai. But as far as I knew, Mark never saw anyone steadily. He fascinated me. He was really nice when you got him talking, which I rarely did, but he was kind of quiet around a lot of people. He actually didn't seem to fit with the other boys. He was smart, kind of preppy, and, well, just nice. Was it so unrealistic to think that someone like him could be interested in someone like me?

I studied myself in the mirror. My auburn hair was straight and full and fell just below my shoulders. I always thought I was average looking, not real pretty, not real ugly, just somewhere in between. The more I thought about Mark, the more excited I got about going. Maybe this party would change everything for me.

I got out of the house fairly easily after I had finally settled on something to wear. Since everybody who was still awake was in the family room, I just went quietly out the front door. I had my own house key, so I didn't worry about getting back in. I had turned the ringer off my phone and put pillows under my covers just in case my dad peeked in on me. The December air chilled me to the bone, though, as I walked down the street to the corner. I only had to wait five minutes, and then Gretchen pulled up.

"This is going to be great! Yahoo!" Gretchen yelled as I jumped into the backseat with Chrissy. Lizzy was up front with Gretchen, and they all were really wound up.

"Yahoo!" yelled Chrissy as the others kept laughing.

"You all are nuts," I said.

"You know it!" Gretchen said. She pulled away from the curb, and off we went.

Mai had most everything done by the time we got there, but we did go and carry chairs up from the basement. When I went to the kitchen I noticed that there was a keg of beer sitting on the floor. I had never had beer. I wondered where they had gotten it and what I was going to do. I should have known they would be drinking. It was pretty foolish of me to think otherwise. I would just wait and see what happened. There was no sense in worrying about it.

People started coming in by the carload. Anybody who was anybody was there. Mark did come, but for the first hour or so I couldn't get anywhere near him. The guys were all kind of clustered around a card table playing some game with coins. Gretchen's clan circled about playing hostess for a while, then decided that they were going to join the guys' game.

"Come on, Bek, let's go play quarters with the guys," Gretchen said and pulled at my arm.

"I'll go get the beers," yelled Mai as we headed over to the table. The guys were all laughing hysterically, shoving at each other. Mark and Jeremy were sitting on the couch, and Gretchen pulled me over there with her. She shooed Mark to one end of the couch and Jeremy to the other, and we sat between them. I felt super uncomfortable, but I managed to smile and say hi to Mark. He grinned back and returned the hello. I was elated.

Mai returned a few moments later with two beers in each hand. They passed them around. One was placed in my hand. I discreetly sniffed it. It smelled pretty gross. I noticed that Mark didn't have a beer. His looked like soda. I thought about going to get a soda instead, too, but everyone else was drinking, and since this was the first time I was ever invited, I thought it would look bad.

"Okay, I'm sure you all know the rules. Since this is your initiation, Beka, you go first," Jeremy said as he reached across Gretchen and handed me a quarter.

"But I, uh, don't know how to play," I said awkwardly.

"Let Mark start, and we'll go around the other way until she gets the idea," Gretchen said quickly. I was grateful to get off the hook.

"Okay, Beka, you try to get the quarter in the glass by bouncing it. If you miss, you drink; if you get it in, you make someone else drink," Mark explained.

I began noticing that a lot of them chose me to drink after their quarter bounced into the cup. The beer was kind of nasty, but I stopped tasting it after a while. I took a deep breath and decided to try to at least let Mark know that I could be friendly. I leaned over to him and said, "I lose, I drink; they win, and they make me drink. I'm not sure I understand the point."

"There is none," he laughed. "They all just want to get drunk, and since you are new to the scene, they want to see you get drunk."

"I notice that you don't have a beer, though."

"I don't drink," he said and shrugged. "Besides, I have to make sure all these fools get home safely. That's kind of why they keep bringing me even though I don't ever drink with them."

We played for what seemed like forever. I wasn't

very good at the game, and before I knew it one beer was gone, and another one ended up in my hand. Then another and another. At some point, they got tired of quarters and they started some question game. I wasn't very good at that either. Mark talked to me a lot, but mostly about what was going on at the party. He kept asking me if I was feeling okay. A couple of times, he told me that I ought to quit, especially if I had never drunk before. I thought I was fine.

Around one, they all decided to go outside and play in the snow. I stood up to walk and down I went. My legs felt like Jell-O. I couldn't stand on them. Mark grabbed my arm just before I hit the floor. He pulled me back up and sat me on the couch. The room was spinning, and I felt sick to my stomach almost immediately. The others left, but Mark stayed behind.

"Do you want me to drive you home?" he asked.

All I could do was nod. I felt too miserable to even move. I just wanted to stretch out on the couch and go right to sleep. "All right, I'll go tell the others that I'm going to drive you home. I'll come back for them later."

He lifted me off the couch and walked me out to his car and put me in the front seat. Even though I felt terrible, it was really, really nice to be treated so sweetly. My house wasn't far away, so we didn't say much.

"Don't pull up in the driveway; just let me off at the corner," I told him as we approached my house.

"I'm not going to leave you on the corner, Beka."

"No, really, I don't want to wake anyone."

"Well, I'll stop here, but I'm walking you to the door."

I didn't argue with that. He walked me to my house.

The cold air had woken me up a bit. Enough that I could really enjoy being next to Mark. Just the two of us. At the door, he said, "It was good to see you tonight, Beka. I'll see you later, okay? Take care." He reached over and squeezed my upper arm. With that, he walked away.

I stumbled into my house, up the stairs, and straight into bed. But for the first time in a long time I had a smile on my face.

I assumed that no one knew I was gone. When I got up the next day, I had a terrible headache. I never even went downstairs. Lucy came up to see if I wanted breakfast, but I told her I still wasn't feeling well. No one bothered me until noon. The next knock was my father.

"Come in," I called, sitting up in my bed.

"Are you all right? I was worried when we still hadn't seen you." He walked over and sat at the end of my bed.

"I still had a headache and I wasn't hungry. I just wanted to get some extra rest." Actually, the thought of food made my stomach flip over, but I decided to leave that part out.

"Do you think we ought to go to the doctor?"

"Oh, no. I'll be fine. I'm feeling better anyway. I was just about to get in the shower."

"Great," he said with a smile, looking relieved. "Well, we were all talking about taking a ride out to Gabby's place. She has a farm just outside of town and has lots of horses. Anna and Lucy are dying to go. You up for it?"

"I don't think so," I said curtly.

"Beka, what's the problem? Gabby is just a friend from work. Just a friend. You don't have anything to worry about."

"You seemed awfully cozy last night."

He sighed and ran his fingers through his hair. "I'm being honest with you, Beka. I'm not interested in Gabby in that way. She knows it. I'm not ready for anything like that." His eyes welled up almost immediately. "I miss your mom too much," he said, and his voice cracked. He took a deep breath. "She's a really nice person from work. When I learned that she was a believer and had a horse farm, I felt it might be a good thing for Anna, Lucy, and you to get to know her. Anna's been interested in horses since she could talk, and you and Lucy are getting older. I love you all very much, but there are some things that only a woman can really understand. I don't want you all to miss out. And neither does God. When Gabby and I became friends, I really felt like it was God's provision for our family. But I promise you, that's all there is to it."

"Yeah, you say that now, but what if something changes?"

"Then you'll be the first to know, Beka. Can you at least give her a chance?"

I shook my head. I didn't want to know anything about Gabby.

"Well, I'm not going to force you. You can stay here. We'll be home after dinner tonight, so you'll have to fend for yourself. Paul will be around today because he has a paper he's working on. But just remember, you're not to go anywhere. Well, I'll see you later, sweetheart." He reached over and hugged me and walked out the door. I curled back up under my covers. I hated Gabby and I didn't want her near my sisters. But, as usual, I couldn't change anything.

I did finally get up and get a shower. I tried to call Lori several times, and then I remembered that she was away at her grandparents' house this weekend. Then Gretchen called around three.

"Wow, what a party. So, details! What happened with you and Mark last night?"

"Nothing to tell," I answered.

"Nothing? You did go home with him last night, didn't you?"

"Yeah, he drove me home, but that was it."

"Shucks, I was thinking that y'all were hooking up."

"Hooking up? You mean like . . . ?"

"Yeah, haven't you ever made out with a guy?"

"No, not exactly."

"Well, Bek, we've got some work to do. Do you like him?"

"Mark? I don't know. I guess. I mean, I don't even know him."

"Well, you know, he's kind of mysterious. But I'll do my best to find out how he feels."

"Don't do that," I pleaded. "I'll feel so dumb."

"I'll be discreet, I promise."

"Well, what do you mean 'mysterious'?"

"Well, I don't think he's ever dated anyone. And he's always around but no one seems to know that much about him. He's an enigma," she said dramatically.

"So, how are you and Jeremy?" I was desperate to change the subject.

"Oh, fine, fine. As long as that skanky new chick stays away."

I knew she was talking about Lori, and I didn't want to say anything about that situation, so I ducked out of the conversation. "I better go. When are they posting callbacks?"

"Should be first thing Monday morning. I'll meet you by the office, 'kay?"

"Sure thing. See ya." I hung up the phone. I was worried how I was going to manage to be friends with both of them without losing both of them.

I stayed in my room the rest of the day. When everyone got home that night, they were all buzzing about Gabby and the horses and the farm. It made me feel even more ill than I already felt.

On Sunday, I worked in the nursery so that I didn't have to go to Sunday school or listen to the sermon. I rocked babies and tried to avoid conversations. I tried to concentrate on the play to get my mind off everything else, but I couldn't get rid of a nagging thought. If the play didn't change things for me, I couldn't think of anything else that would. And what was I going to do then?

I woke up Monday morning with a sick feeling. It took me a couple of minutes to remember what it was . . . then it hit me. Callbacks would be posted today. Ugh. I had begun thinking that getting a part was my only hope of fixing things without talking, but what were my chances of that? I got ready for school really quickly. By the time I headed downstairs I decided I just wanted to get called back. I thought having the directors think I was good enough to see again would feel great right now. I decided to stop thinking about a part and just wait to see the callback list.

The girls were still really wound up about the horses and the farm when I got downstairs. I ate a bowl of cereal quietly at the counter, waiting anxiously for Paul to get finished. I didn't want to seem anxious, though. Nobody seemed to remember why today was so important to me. Which is what I had wanted. So, why did I feel angry with them for not remembering?

"I thought Pickett was the prettiest horse there," Anna gushed.

"Pickett was pretty," Lucy agreed. "But didn't you like riding Barnaby?"

"Sure," Anna said and nodded. "But I want to be able to ride Pickett."

"Anna, Gabby said you could ride Pickett someday. You just have to practice a lot more before you're ready to ride one of the big horses," Lucy reminded her.

"Daddy, can we go out to Gabby's house every day so that I can practice riding?"

"Gabby has a business to run, Miracle. She can't help you every day." Dad laughed. "But we'll work out something so that you can keep practicing."

Anna seemed satisfied with his response. But I hated that Anna wanted to spend time out there. Even though I knew it was probably mostly because of the horses, I didn't want any of them near Gabby.

Paul finally finished his breakfast and headed for the door. I grabbed my stuff and followed him. He didn't say anything on the ride there. I debated asking him about his paper or something. Just to break the ice. But I didn't. I just sat there silently too.

I headed straight for the office. I didn't even stop at my locker. I could feel my heart pounding in my chest. I turned the corner and saw a small crowd of people hud-

dled around the window of the office. I stopped. I didn't
want to go see the list in front of all those people. I
turned to head back down the hallway when I heard my
name being screamed.

"Beka, Beka!"

I turned around and saw Gretchen motioning to me
to come to her. I slowly headed back towards the office.
When I got there she grabbed my arm and pulled and
pushed us towards the front of the crowd. She pointed at
the list.

"Look!" she said. "You got called back. So did I! Isn't
this great!" She hugged me and jumped back through the
crowd. I couldn't believe it. But there it was—Rebekah
Madison—in black-and-white. I pushed through the crowd
to let others get a look at the list and headed to my locker
in a daze. Lori was waiting for me when I got there.

"So, what happened? I didn't try to push through that
crowd up there."

"I got called back. I guess that's good," I said, still in
shock.

"Good? That's wonderful."

"Yeah, but that means I have to audition again
today."

"So what," she said and smiled. "You obviously did
good the first time. You'll do fine."

I took a deep breath. The whole school was talking
about the callback list and what they thought would happen. I overheard several mentions of my name, but mostly they were saying they were surprised my name was on
the list. I tried not to listen to any of it, but it was hard to
keep my mind on my schoolwork. I tracked down Paul

after lunch to remind him that I had permission to stay after school.

"No problem. I'll come back around five to pick you up." He paused and smiled. "I saw your name on the call-back list. Congratulations!"

I smiled and nodded, but I couldn't say anything. I was glad he was happy for me, but getting called back was only half of it. There was still only a chance that I would get a part. I talked with Gretchen in journalism. She was so wound up about getting Annie.

"So what's going to happen today?" I asked her after she had calmed down and finished explaining to me why she had a chance to get Annie.

"Well, I'm not sure. It depends on what they're still not sure about." She shrugged.

"That helps," I said sarcastically.

She laughed. "Well, we'll just have to wait and see. We've only got twenty more minutes to wait. Meet me by the stage door after the bell."

She waltzed off to go talk with the girls at the computer. I just sat there making myself more and more nervous, all the way up to the sound of the final bell ringing. I went to my locker first and got my books and then headed back towards the auditorium. Gretchen was waiting there when I turned the corner.

"Quick, Beka. They want to see us all onstage. They're going to tell us how it's all going to work," she said as she pulled me onto the stage.

About twenty kids were gathered on the stage. Everything was lit so we could see all the way to the back of the auditorium.

In front of the students stood Mr. Thompson and Mr. Stickel. They were both going to be directing the play. Thompson did more of the music side while Mr. Stickel did more of the acting side.

"All right. I know you all are excited, but we are going to take this nice and slow this afternoon. We may ask you to read from the script, sing again, or just stand onstage with someone else. We are looking at many different things today to help us make our decision. The cast list will be posted tomorrow morning by the office. Rehearsals will begin the day we get back from winter break. We will go from three to five P.M. each day until the play in March. There may also be some Saturday afternoon dance rehearsals. If anyone here cannot commit to these things, tell me now.

"All right then. Mark Floyd and Greg Baskin, please remain on the stage. I would like everybody else to wait out in the hallway area. We'll call you when we need you."

With that we turned and left for the hallway. I looked around to see where Mark was, but I wasn't tall enough to see. I hadn't even known he auditioned. It made me want to get a part all the more. An excuse to spend every afternoon with him. Wow!

Off and on, Gretchen or I would get called back out onto the stage. Once they asked me to sing again, and once I had to just stand there with about five other girls in a row, including Gretchen. And that was it. The rest of the time we sat around and waited. Mark sat at the other end of the hall from us reading a book, so I didn't ever talk to him. We were all finished by 4:30, which left me with half an hour to wait for Paul. I said good-bye to Gretchen and went to wait for Paul out in front of the school.

The cold air felt good at first. I sat on the curb and thought about *Annie,* Mark, my family, Christmas. Everything was so quiet and still. It felt nice.

"Hey, Beka, what are you doing sitting out here?"

I turned my head to see Mark headed straight for me. My heart immediately started thumping in my throat.

"Waiting for my ride." I smiled. "I, uh, didn't know you had auditioned."

"Yeah, I do every year." He returned the smile as he sat down next to me. "So, how'd you feel Saturday morning?"

"Don't remind me." I sighed. "That was the first time I ever drank."

"Why did you?"

"Why did I what? Drink? I don't know. It seemed like the thing to do."

Mark shook his head. "I hope you didn't drink because that's what everybody else was doing. You need to be who you are despite what everybody else is doing."

I sat silently. In a way I felt like Paul or my dad was lecturing me, but I also felt embarrassed. I knew I wasn't a strong person, and I felt like he saw me as a weakling with no mind of my own. And the worst part about it was that I agreed with him.

"Look, I'm not trying to lecture you. I just hate to see that crowd drag someone else into their meaningless, shallow world."

"But isn't that your world too?"

"No," he said emphatically. "I try to be a friend, to be something steady in their sea of confusion, but I am not a part of them. I am my own person, and they know that. They know that they can't manipulate or pull me into their . . . I don't know what you would call it . . . choices."

I didn't know how to respond. He sounded so sure of himself. So confident. It made me feel more insecure than I already was. How could I feel confident and sure about myself and my decisions? I felt ashamed for the way I had acted, but in a way, I wasn't unhappy about the attention it had brought from Mark.

Mark stood up after a few moments. "Look, Beka, I know I don't know you very well, and I know I have no right to tell you what you should or shouldn't do. But you seem like a nice girl. Don't become one of them." He bent down and squeezed my shoulder. "I'll see you tomorrow, okay?" He smiled a wide, sincere smile. I nodded and smiled back, but I felt like such a child. How could someone like him ever be interested in someone like me?

Home was very quiet. At least the area around me was. Same old stuff from everybody else. They were happy and excited about various things, and I just sat quietly through dinner, sat quietly in the living room with them for a while, and then excused myself to do homework. I felt like an alien. I didn't speak their language, and it seemed like when I wasn't fighting with them, I was in this isolation zone. I couldn't stop it. I told myself I didn't care, but my heart ached. I felt so alone.

I talked to Lori briefly because she wanted to know about callbacks, but even though I felt lonely, I didn't really want to talk to her either. I went to bed thinking that if I didn't get a part in the play, I might as well just disappear off the face of the earth. It probably wouldn't make much difference to anybody else.

The next morning, I was very anxious to get to school, but everybody seemed to be going in slow motion. Anna spilled her bowl of cereal and then Lucy spilled juice on her white blouse so she needed to go change. And, of course, I snapped at both of them for being clumsy and lectured them on being more careful, but I was so preoccupied that their hurt expressions barely registered until later that day. Paul was running later than usual, and he is never late for anything. I briefly wondered if they were trying to get back at me. I knew in my head that it was probably just a coincidence, but I was so irritated by the time I got in the car that I was ready to blow a gasket.

"Crazy morning, huh?"

I didn't even respond. I wanted to ask what took him so long, but I knew I couldn't ask nicely, so I just kept my mouth shut. He didn't say anything else on the ride to school until we got to the parking lot.

"I hope everything turns out well for you today."

So he did realize today was a big day. It helped squelch my mood a little to know that he was thinking about me. I headed straight for the office, as nervous as I had ever been in my life. There were some people milling around, but no crowd around the window like yesterday. As soon as I got close I saw why. There was a sign in the office window that said, "Cast list will be posted at 3:00 P.M. today."

The day was torture. My irritation returned immediately, and everything seemed to go wrong. Gretchen was full of herself as usual and kept making snide remarks about her "competitors," though she really didn't see anyone as competition. I was beginning to hope that anybody *but* Gretchen would get the part of Annie. Lori listened as I complained about Gretchen, but she also seemed to be dropping hints about coming to my house to meet the rest of my family, and she kept asking me why I was friends with Gretchen if I didn't like her. I got frustrated because I didn't know what to say to her.

When the final bell rang, I didn't rush to the office with the other girls from my journalism class. I walked slowly down the hall and stopped at my locker, savoring the idea that I could have a part. Because I knew that once I saw the list, there would be no more dreaming about the what-ifs, only reality.

Bʋt I never even made it to the office. From the end of the hallway I could see Gretchen jumping. I was sure she had gotten Annie. When she spotted me she took off at a sprint. But I could hear her from where I stood.

"I got Annie!" She reached me and grabbed my shoulders. "You got Molly. Isn't that great! Your first year auditioning and you got a part! We get to be orphans together!" She hugged me and went running and jumping back down the hallway to receive her praise.

I breathed deeply, a little shocked. I was happy, but it didn't seem real. I had gotten a part in the play. It wasn't one of the major, major parts, but it was a speaking part.

I wouldn't be just standing around and dancing with the chorus. But I felt awkward about going home. I knew they would ask about what happened, but I had been so awful, I didn't feel like they should be happy for me or anything.

I walked to the car. I could see Paul in the front seat waiting for me, getting the car warmed up. As I opened the door, he grinned at me.

"Congratulations!" he said enthusiastically. "You must be happy."

"Sure." I shrugged. I didn't want to seem overly excited, but I hadn't meant to seem completely unenthusiastic. Paul's grin quickly faded, and he didn't try to make any more conversation. I felt terrible. It would have been the perfect opportunity to break the ice with him, and I blew it. And there was no going back. We drove home in silence.

I couldn't figure out why I wasn't excited. I mean, I was happy about the part. But I felt kind of embarrassed, and I didn't want to talk to my family about it. I really didn't think they understood anyway; they were just being polite and supportive. No one else in the family ever did anything with plays.

I never brought the play up at home, but Paul put me on the spot in front of everyone at dinner. "Beka has some news," he said simply.

They all looked at me expectantly. Paul kept eating. I couldn't figure out if he had done it to encourage me to talk or if he was getting back at me. I felt so awkward.

"I got a part in the play at school," I mumbled. The table erupted in a chorus of "Congratulations" and "That's great" and questions all at the same time.

After a few minutes, Dad quieted everybody down when he saw I wasn't going to respond to everyone all at once.

"Tell us about it, Beka," he said when everyone had resumed eating their dinners. They were all waiting to hear, though, with their eyes still on me.

I took a deep breath. I would just give the basics. I figured that would satisfy them. "I got the part of Molly. She's one of the orphans," I said, looking up only briefly. "It's not a big part or anything," I added when they didn't say anything.

"Can I come see your play, Beka?" Anna asked.

"We'll all go see the play, Anna," Dad told her. "That's great. When do you have to start practicing?"

"After Christmas break," I answered, relaxing a little bit. "We'll have rehearsal every day after school and some Saturdays."

"It is a good part, even if it's not one of the main ones," Lucy said carefully. "You have lines and songs to sing. You even get to sing by yourself a couple of times, I think."

I nodded in response, but I was curious as to how she knew so much about the play. Later that night, it hit me. She used to go to plays with Mom. She must have seen it sometime with her. Mom tried to take each of us out by ourselves every so often, and that's one of the things that Lucy and Mom seemed to do most often. They had even traveled some good distances to see some shows. The dinner conversation about the play eventually tapered off, and I escaped to my room without too much fuss.

Gretchen called around seven just to gush some more about getting Annie.

"I just can't believe it. I am so excited. We are going to have so much fun!"

"I'm excited too. You know, I never looked at the list. Did Chrissy, Mai, or Lizzy get a part?"

"Yeah, well, Chrissy is just one of the extra orphans. The ones with no lines. She's bummed. But Mai is Pepper, and Lizzy has a speaking part in the Hooverville scene."

"The Hooverville scene. What's that?"

"It's when Annie, I mean, it's when I am running through the streets and I meet a bunch of bums. Didn't you read the play?"

"Most of it. I skimmed through it. I forgot about that scene."

"Guess what else? Your Marky-poo got a part too. Ahhh, a stage romance. I can see it now."

"Please, don't call him Marky-poo," I pleaded. "There is absolutely nothing going on. What part did he get?"

"He got a lead. He's going to be Rooster. Miss Hannigan's brother."

"Really? Isn't Rooster a bad guy? Mark's so nice. I can't see him being Rooster."

"Mark's so nice," she cooed back at me. "Do you hear yourself? You have it bad; you just won't admit it. I forgot to follow up on our Mystery Man. Let me make a few phone calls and I'll call you back."

"No, please don't," I protested. But the line went dead, and I was sure that she was already dialing me into complete embarrassment.

About twenty minutes later, the phone rang again.

"Gretchen, please tell me you didn't embarrass me," I said, not even waiting for her hello.

"Well, I'm sure I didn't embarrass you, but this isn't Gretchen."

It was Mark. I didn't need Gretchen to embarrass me. I seemed to be doing just fine on my own.

"Uh, sorry Mark. I thought it was Gretchen calling back, and I never expected you to call me or anything. I mean, I didn't even know you had this phone number." I knew I was babbling, but I didn't know what to say.

"Well, actually, I called your family's number first. Your sister gave me this number." That meant that they would all know a guy had called me. I just hoped they would forget about it by morning. Most of the girls my age had steady boyfriends already. I felt so backward.

"So, how is Gretchen embarrassing you?"

"Uh, well, it's nothing. Just silly girl stuff. You wouldn't be interested."

"So, do you and Gretchen hang out a lot together?"

"Well, sometimes, I guess. She's the one who convinced me to try out for the play."

"Actually, that's why I called. Congratulations on your part. You'll make a great Molly."

"Thanks," I said sincerely. "And congratulations to you, as well. So you're playing our bad guy, huh?"

"Yeah. I'm looking forward to it. Well, the other reason I wanted to call was to invite you to my house Friday night. I'm having a dinner party for those members of the cast who would like to celebrate without drinking and throwing up all night. I'm sure Gretchen and Jeremy will arrange the alternative, but I thought I'd give you a choice."

"I'd like to come. But I don't have a way to get there. I mean, I have a car; I'm just not allowed to use it until next week."

"Did you get in trouble last Saturday?"

"No, it was something else."

"Well, you don't live that far from me. If you don't mind coming a little early, I can come get you."

"Really? You wouldn't mind?"

"On one condition. You have to promise me you won't go to the drinking party after we're finished at my house."

"Okay, I mean, what do you think I am, an alcoholic? I told you last week that was my first time drinking."

"I know. And I believe you, but as I said yesterday, I'd hate to see you get caught up in the endless party cycle."

"Okay, well, that sounds fine."

"All right. I'll come get you around six on Friday if that's all right."

"Great." I couldn't believe it.

"Well, I'll see you in school tomorrow, okay? Bye."

I hung up with my heart still pounding in my chest. The phone rang again about thirty seconds after I hung up.

"What do you have against call waiting?" Gretchen demanded.

"I'm lucky to have this phone line, Gretchen. I don't want to push it, okay?"

"All right. All right. Who have you been on the phone with?"

"Mark," I said simply. I had to move the phone away from my ear when she screamed into the receiver.

"That's incredible! I was just talking to Jeremy about him. He called you?"

"Yeah. I was shocked. I thought it was you calling back."

"So, what happened?"

"Well," I began. I didn't want her to know about my promise to Mark, but I wanted to tell her about the party. "He invited me to his house Friday night for his cast/dinner party."

"Oh. Are you going to go? He won't have any beer there, so we were talking about maybe going there and having a real party somewhere else afterwards. You can just come with us when it's over, and we can have some real fun."

"So you are going to go to Mark's?"

"Sure," she answered. "I think he invited the whole cast. Jeremy told me about it earlier. I was wondering if he was going to call to invite you or just mention it in school. Well, anyway, Jeremy says that Mark is the kind of guy who does his own thing. He doesn't drink or smoke or date, but he's a good guy. They all like him even though he's different."

"You didn't say anything about me, did you?"

"How uncouth do you think I am? I just inquired about him. He's only been here two years and he didn't start hanging out with the other guys until last year. I just sounded casually curious, I promise."

"All right. I'm not sure it matters anyway. He's nice to everybody. He's not treating me any differently."

"Well, maybe not yet, but give him some time. You weren't even on his radar screen till last week. Hey, regardless of where we party Friday after Mark's, I'm having some of the girls over for a sleepover Saturday night. Since this is our last week of school, and next week is Christmas, we need to do something fun with just us girls."

We talked for a few more minutes and then hung up. Lori called a while later to say congratulations. We didn't talk long. I really felt bad because I knew I was her only friend and I was making all these plans that I couldn't include her in.

I wasn't sure what to do. I couldn't believe how much had changed in just a week. School was becoming a refuge in some ways, but I felt pushed and pulled there too. I didn't know how I was going to get out of Gretchen's party. I didn't know how to do anything with Lori. And my feelings for Mark had sprung from a seedling to a tree overnight. I suspected that he was just being a nice guy, even though I kept trying to convince myself that I had hope. Then there was the problem of convincing my dad to let me go out all weekend. He would not be thrilled about my plans. I went to bed with my head spinning.

School was abuzz about the cast list, but the day was pretty uneventful. I had several classes with Mark, and he always smiled, but he never talked to me. I was bummed about it. I had dreamed that he had sent me little notes all day long. I had woken up with more expectation than I had realized. I could tell Lori was feeling put out when I turned down an invitation to go to her house on Saturday. I told her I had things to do this weekend, but I knew I couldn't put her off much longer. I did want to hang out with her, but at the same time I didn't want to feel personally responsible for her. I kind of wished she would make some other friends.

I bided my time that night to ask Dad about that weekend. Paul had driven Lucy to youth group and Anna was playing in her room, so Dad was all by himself when I went into the family room. He was reading a book, but he closed it and took off his glasses as soon as I came in. I felt really intimidated about talking to him. Especially about having to ask him for something when I hadn't been very nice lately.

"Hey, Butterfly." He smiled. "I thought you were doing your homework upstairs."

"Uh, yeah, I finished it," I said as I sat down on the far end of the couch away from the recliner he was sitting in. "I, uh, wanted to ask you something."

"Sure. What do you have on your mind?"

"When you grounded me last week, I know I lost my car for two weeks, but I only had to stay in last weekend, right?"

He sat back in his chair. "Yes, that's right. Did you want to go somewhere this weekend?"

"One of the guys from the cast is having a cast party Friday night. It's a dinner party."

"Well, do you have a way to get there and back? Your curfew is still eleven."

"Yeah, I have a ride."

"Well, that sounds fine. Please be sure you leave the number of where you are so that I can reach you."

I nodded and stood up. I didn't know whether to ask about Saturday now or later. Since I had his attention, I thought I might as well get it over with. I sat back down. "I also got invited to a sleepover for Saturday night at a friend's house."

"Friday and Saturday night? Don't you think that's a little much?"

"No. I haven't done anything with friends for months. I never even went to any parties before . . . I just want to celebrate the end of school and the play with my friends." I wasn't yelling, but I had raised my voice. My dad had listened quietly, and he remained silent for several minutes after I had finished.

"Well, I'm going to need to think about the Saturday night thing. What about church?"

"I really don't want to go," I mumbled.

"Well, I'm going to need to think and pray about this. I'll let you know when I decide."

"Whatever," I said quietly and walked out of the room. It was so frustrating! Why couldn't he have just said yes or no like a normal parent? It was true I hadn't asked to go anywhere for a long time, except dinner at Lori's last week. I knew his argument would be that I need to spend more time with the family, but I didn't want to do that. I was spending most of my time in my room when I was home. So what did it matter if I was home at all? I knew that there was no use in saying anything else to Dad until he made his decision. I should have argued my point better. At least I was going to be able to go to Mark's, and Dad hadn't said a word about it being at a guy's house.

By Thursday, I was mad. Dad had still not said anything, and I knew bringing it up would be the kiss of death. Gretchen had been on my case for two days asking if I was coming. I felt like an idiot telling her over and over that I didn't know yet. It wasn't until Friday morning, the eleventh hour, that he finally approached me.

"Beka, I've been meaning to get back to you about your weekend plans," he said as he sat next to me at the kitchen table. I looked up from my cereal but didn't respond.

"I'm willing to make a deal with you. I understand you feel that you haven't done anything with friends for a long time, and I agree with you. I feel it would be good for you to spend time with friends."

"Then why—" I began to protest.

"Wait," he said, holding up a hand. "I'm not finished yet. I also feel that you are not spending enough time with the family. I want you to be able to do both things in balance. So, what I am proposing is this: I will allow you to go to both of your events this weekend if you will come with the family out to the farm on Sunday afternoon. We aren't leaving until one, so that gives you plenty of time to get back here. How does that sound?"

"Gabby's farm?" I asked through clenched teeth.

"Yes, the girls want to go back out there, and I thought we could all go out to dinner after we finished. Paul is free, so the whole family will be together."

"Gabby's not family."

"First of all, she's not coming to dinner with us. Second, I have already explained that to you. Do you not believe me?"

I thought about that for a minute. My dad had never lied to me, but I guess I thought that he wanted it to be an innocent friendship and was in denial about what was really going on. I trusted him, but I didn't trust her. When I didn't respond, he stood up and asked, "Well, are you willing to spend Sunday with the family?"

"I don't really have a choice, do I? To get what I want, I have to do what you want me to do. Fine, whatever, I'll go, but I'm not going to pretend to be happy about it."

"That wasn't the reaction I was hoping for," he said sadly. But he turned and walked away without saying anything else. I left for school feeling deflated.

After the play announcement the week had been anticlimactic. Even though it was the last day, and a ten-day vacation lay before us, not to mention the party and sleepover, I wasn't in the least bit excited. Mark hadn't really said anything all week, leaving me with the feeling I had been making up any signals. Things weren't going well with Lori either. I had to think of something I could do with her soon. And Gretchen was just so bossy and full of herself that I didn't even know why I wanted to go to her house.

I had decided to try to straighten things out with Lori at lunch, but once we were in the cafeteria I found it difficult to form the words. Especially since Lori was still being friendly and nice, even though I had been kind of distant.

"So, what are your winter break plans?" she asked soon after we sat down.

"I don't know." I shrugged. "Not much, I guess. What about you?"

"Well, we are staying around here. You know, the adoption may be finalized in a few weeks. I can still hardly believe I have a family."

Lori had been telling me about how the Rollinses had moved forward on the adoption. She was so open with me about her feelings about the whole thing, but I had such a hard time being open with her. I knew I could trust her, but I hadn't said anything to anybody for so long that I felt like I had forgotten how. I thought maybe if I started small that it would get the ball rolling.

"I'm so happy that you are going to have a family. I haven't been doing so well with mine lately. That's kind of why I haven't asked you over."

"Oh," she said quietly. "Do you want to talk about it?"

"If I could explain, I would. I just don't know. It's like sour milk. You can't tell when it went sour, but you know when it is."

"Is there anything I can do?"

"No, but I guess it helps that you know."

"You know, it's hard to not have a mom to talk to, as we both know. Megan asks about you all the time. I'm sure she'd be more than happy to talk with you. Maybe she'd even have some advice on smoothing things out with your family."

"I don't know. I only met her that one night at your house."

"But don't you see, that sometimes makes things easier. She's an impartial party. When I was having problems with my mom, Liz, my social worker, was really helpful to me. I think it's easier to spill your guts to someone who isn't involved."

"Well, you have a point. Tell you what, I'll think about it."

"Can't ask for more than that." She grinned. After we finished up lunch, I promised I would call her the following week. I felt better about talking with her and was reminded how much nicer Lori was than Gretchen. I knew who would be a better friend, but I wasn't willing to give up the excitement surrounding Gretchen and the play. It kept my mind off my mess.

Later, in journalism class, Gretchen filled me in on the plans for the evening.

"Okay, we're all going to Mark's at 6:30. Since it's a dinner thing, we figure we'll be out of there by nine. Then off to Jeremy's for a real party," she said quickly. "Do you need a ride to Mark's?"

"No," I answered.

"Cool—did you get your car back?"

"Not exactly," I said. "Mark is going to pick me up."

"What! You're holding out on me! What happened? Is it like a date thing?"

"No, no, no! He just offered to give me a ride when he invited me to the party."

"Sounds pretty close to a date. We'll have to light a fire under that boy. We'll take care of that Saturday," she said with a big grin.

I had no idea what she meant by that, but I was more worried about how I was going to get out of going to Jeremy's. She just assumed I would go with them, but it wasn't just my promise to Mark. I knew I had better be home no later than 10:59 or I was going to get grounded again. No one at Jeremy's party would get me home by that time. So even if I had wanted to go, I didn't see how I could.

Mark came up from behind me and put his arm around my shoulder as I was walking to my locker after the final bell. He smiled one of the most beautiful smiles I had ever seen.

"I'll come get you at six, right?"

I nodded dreamily. He could have said anything and I probably would have just agreed. Just as quickly he was gone. I couldn't wait till six.

I went straight to my room

when I got home and stayed put. I was thrilled that I
didn't have to eat dinner downstairs. I changed outfits
four times. I didn't know whether to dress up or be casual. I finally settled on a sweater and skirt. Casual, yet dis-
tinctive. I pulled and pushed at my hair for a good bit of
time too. Eventually I ended up with part of it up and
part of it down. Then I waited. I wasn't sure if Mark was
going to come to the door or not. I was kind of hoping I
could just leave when I saw him pull up and avoid my
father. Because of that, I headed downstairs at 5:45 to
keep an eye out for him.

Just before six, Mark's black Celica pulled into the

driveway. I turned to go yell good-bye to Dad and leave, but there he was standing right beside me.

"Just wait, Beka. Let him come to the door. I want to meet him," Dad said calmly.

My heart sank. "Please, Dad, it's not a date or any-thing. Just let me go." Before I even got finished speak-ing, the doorbell rang. I reluctantly followed my father to the front foyer.

"Hello, Mr. Madison," Mark said confidently as he shook my father's hand.

"Nice to meet you—Mark, is it?"

"Yes, sir, Mark Floyd."

"So, this party is at your house?"

"Yes, sir. My parents are hosting it for the cast."

"Rebekah has to be back by eleven. Will you be bringing her home?"

"I'll have her back on time, sir."

"Okay, well, have fun. Good-bye, sweetheart. I'll see you later. It was nice meeting you, Mark."

"You too, sir." They shook hands again, and I closed the door behind me.

"I'm so sorry, Mark. I tried to get out of there before you had to come to the door."

"No, it's fine. I understand. If you were my daughter, I'd want to meet me too."

"I know, but I did explain to him that it wasn't . . . that you were . . . I mean, that . . ."

"Beka, stop. It's perfectly fine." He grinned.

I relaxed back into the seat. I knew that he was just giving me a ride a few miles down the road. But it felt like a date. Since I had never been on one, it was the closest thing I had ever experienced. And it felt so nice to be sitting in a car beside him. He looked great too. He was wearing a soft knit sweater with dress slacks.

"You look really nice tonight, Beka," he said after a few moments.

"Thank you," I said shyly. I didn't know what to say after that, but a few minutes later we pulled up into his driveway. He lived in a huge pale yellow house. There was lots of land around it. I had seen the house before, but I had never been inside. It was really beautiful.

"Mom, Dad, this is Rebekah Madison. Beka, this is my mom and dad," he introduced us when we reached the kitchen. It was a bustle of activity, but they both stopped to shake hands with me.

"Rebekah, it's good to meet you," his mom said and smiled briefly. "I was so sorry to read about your mom earlier this year."

"Thank you," I said. "It's nice to meet you too. Can I help with anything?"

They put me to work finishing up the salad. I was grateful for the distraction. I kept glancing over at Mark, who was cutting loaves of fresh-baked bread, just to remind myself that I was really there. Once, he caught my glance and smiled warmly. My heart made a puddle on the floor.

Before long, the doorbell started ringing and we were seating people at the tables. I felt like I could have been his girlfriend as I helped to serve and work with his family. Mark made sure I had a place near him, which made me feel wonderful. Gretchen kept grinning at me every time she saw me or Mark look at each other. She mouthed, "We'll talk later," during dinner.

I barely tasted dinner, and even though Mark and I didn't talk a lot during dinner, he was near me. And that's all that seemed to matter. I decided to just tell Gretchen I couldn't go to Jeremy's and not get into why. I hoped she would listen. Once we got all of the dishes cleared, everybody went into the living room where they had games laid out. Different groups gathered around different games. I jumped up to help clear and went into the kitchen to help clean up.

"Aren't you a dear, Beka," his mom said when she saw me rinsing dishes. "Thank you for helping."

"No problem," I smiled. "I'm glad to help."

Once the kitchen was under control, Mark took my hand and gently pulled me into the living room where most people had gathered, and we joined a game of Blurt! I was so thrilled to be sitting near Mark that I barely noticed it when Gretchen and a group of others stood up and began gathering coats to leave. Gretchen came over and tapped me on the shoulder.

"You ready to go, Bek?"

Mark leaned back on his arm and looked at me but didn't say anything.

"I, um, well, I think I'm going to stay here," I said as I fiddled with my sweater.

Gretchen didn't say anything. She turned to Mark and said thank you and then left. Mark patted my back as he turned back to the game to see whose turn it was. I could tell by the look on Gretchen's face that she was mad. I wasn't sure yet what that meant for me, but I knew it couldn't be good.

People started dispersing quickly after Gretchen and her group had left. I helped clean up the games and took cups to the kitchen. After a while, only Rob, Stacy, and I were left with Mark. I soon found out why they were still hanging around. Mark was going to give them a ride home too. I was disappointed. I had hoped that since the evening had started like a date, maybe it would end like one too. Those thoughts about Mark just being nice were at war with the hopes that he was really interested in me. I hoped that maybe he would drop off Stacy and Rob first, and then we would have a few minutes alone. I quickly realized, though, that Mark was headed for my house first. I felt so deflated. He pulled into my driveway and got out with me to walk me to the door.

"I'm glad you came tonight. And I'm not trying to sound condescending, but I'm proud of you for not going to the other party."

"Yeah, well, thanks for giving me a ride and for inviting me," I said without emotion. I was feeling really dumb for reading more into his actions than I should have.

"I hope you have a good break and a great Christmas," he said, smiling, as we reached the door.

"You too," I muttered. I couldn't muster a smile. I knew in my head that I should have smiled and been friendlier to show him that I liked him, but I couldn't make my face do what I wanted it to do. I was feeling terrible and I knew it showed on my face.

"See ya," he said and waved as he climbed into the

car. I stood on the porch for a few more minutes getting more and more angry with myself for making Gretchen mad in order to please Mark, who obviously didn't seem to notice the sacrifice much. All of a sudden I was overwhelmed with the urge to go to that party. I still couldn't drive my car, but after saying good night to Dad and making a few phone calls, I finally tracked down Gretchen. She was mad at first, but I explained that I had to come home and then sneak back out in order to go to the party. She was annoyed that she had to come get me, but she agreed to come pick me up. I hung up the phone with satisfaction. Maybe a few drinks would help me forget about Mark.

Within thirty minutes, I had snuck out of the house and was sitting in Jeremy's basement drinking a beer. Last week, I had felt nervous and unsure about drinking, but as I sipped at my beer, I felt vindicated. I still wanted Mark to be there to take care of me, but I knew there was no chance of him showing up at the party. He had made his feelings clear. There weren't many people at the party I knew. And those that I knew were pretty engrossed in each other. So I just kept drinking, willing myself into an alternate reality. It wasn't long before everybody sounded really funny and the room looked a bit lopsided. Then, the next thing I knew, I was waking up with a pounding headache and an incredible urge to throw up.

I got up slowly from the couch, trying to get my legs to work. I used the furniture to work my way across the room. I opened three doors before I found the bathroom, and I barely made it to the toilet. I had never felt so sick in my life. After I had finished, I looked at myself in the mirror. I was a mess. My hair was everywhere, my make-up was smeared, and I looked a little gray. I walked back out into the family room and carefully stepped over the bodies strewn all over the basement. I didn't see anyone awake. Then I looked at my watch and panicked. It was six A.M. I woke up some very cranky people as I desperately tried to find Gretchen. I finally found her wedged behind a recliner next to Jeremy.

"Gretchen, Gretchen, you have to wake up, you have to drive me home. I'm sorry. I'm so sorry. But you have to help me."

She opened her eyes a crack.

"Go back to sleep, Beka. We'll go home later."

"Later is not going to work. I snuck out, remember? My whole family is going to be up soon. My brother probably is already up."

"Beka, I'm not getting up. I'm tired and I don't feel well. Go away!"

My heart, which had already been pounding, was now at a frantic pace. I looked around for a familiar face. I spotted Theresa curled up by the fireplace. I went over to her and gently shook her. I didn't know her that well, but she was really nice at the auditions, and I was desperate.

"Theresa, Theresa. Can you help me? I need a ride home right away."

She stirred and rubbed her eyes.

"What time is it?"

"Six."

"Oh, my!" She exclaimed. "I need to get home. Oh, my goodness, my parents are going to kill me."

"Can you take me home? Please?"

"Yeah, but we have to leave right this second."

I found my shoes and coat and was waiting at the bottom of the stairs within minutes. We stumbled up the stairs. Now that I knew I was going to get home, I felt sick all over again, and my head felt like a jackhammer was pounding away on it. It had snowed a little bit overnight. Theresa and I both slipped and fell as we ran to her car. She had a hard time maneuvering it in between all the other cars jammed into the backyard. Soon, though, we were on our way. She sped the whole way. I was worried she was going to be pulled over. I could still smell beer and smoke on our clothes. Before she had even pulled into my driveway, I could see all of our vehicles and one single police car in our driveway. I was in trouble!

"Wow! Your dad must have really flipped out," Theresa said sympathetically as she pulled into the driveway right behind the blue-and-white police car. "Good luck."

I got out of the car quickly but then just stood in the driveway. I was terrified to walk into my house. Terrified but also embarrassed and angry. I assumed there was no reason to try to sneak in, so I climbed the stairs to the back porch slowly. Through the window on the back door, I could see the back of the police officer, Paul, and my dad facing them. They were all talking, but they all turned towards me as I opened the back door. For a moment, we all just stared at each other. Then they erupted.

"Where have you been?" my father demanded. I had never seen him so angry. His face was tense and red.

"We have been looking everywhere for you, calling everywhere for you," Paul added harshly.

"Well, young lady, I'm glad you're back safe and sound." The officer turned and looked at my dad. "I guess I'll be going, Mr. Madison. Let me know if I can do anything else for you." He closed his notebook and walked past me to the door.

The silence in the room was deafening. Lucy walked into the kitchen a few minutes later but turned and walked out when she saw all of us standing there. After a few minutes, Dad turned to Paul.

"Paul, can you give us a few minutes? I need to speak with Beka alone."

Paul nodded and left the room, leaving my father and me staring at each other.

"You smell like beer and smoke. Have you been drinking and smoking?"

"Yes," I said firmly. I didn't bother to tell him I hadn't smoked. I figured at this point, it really didn't matter.

"Why? Why would you do something like this? Sneak out of the house? Stay out all night? Drinking and smoking?" His voice was anxious, but it wasn't raised. I just shrugged my shoulders. That's when his volume went back up.

"That is *not* an answer, young lady. I want to know why you would do something to completely destroy the trust I have always had in you."

"I wanted to go to the party, so I went. I knew you would say no, so I didn't tell you." I was surprised at my own calmness. I knew I had been wrong, but I wasn't about to let my dad know that I was scared. And it gave me some satisfaction to know that I was making him angrier by not reacting. We stared at each other for a few more minutes.

"Go to your room. Get yourself cleaned up. We will talk later."

"Maybe I don't want to talk to you about anything," I said as I brushed past him and headed for the stairs. As soon as the words came out of my mouth, I regretted them. I wanted to hurt him, but I also wanted to just sink into his arms and let go. Why did I choose to hurt him and make things worse?

I barely made it to my room before the tears began. I dropped onto my bed and sobbed. I was so angry with myself for making things so bad. And I knew, beyond a shadow of a doubt, that my father meant what he said about not trusting me anymore. My heart was racing from the panic that rose up inside of me. I felt so trapped and so alone. As I tried to regain my composure, all that kept going through my head was that I wanted to die. I just didn't want to face anybody or anything anymore. I knew that it would be the worst thing I could do. I thought about my family. Even though I thought they would be glad to be rid of me, I knew in my heart that it wasn't true. But I couldn't get the thoughts of dying out of my head. It seemed the only way to escape everything.

I awoke with a start when there was a knock at my door. I couldn't even muster the words "come in." I just sat up on my bed and pulled a pillow into my lap. My father's face appeared as my door opened slowly.

"May I come in?" he asked.

I shrugged. I just couldn't form the words in my mouth. My mouth felt dry and my face felt swollen. I wondered briefly about what I must have looked like, but it didn't seem to matter.

My father pulled the chair over from my desk and sat near my bed. He sighed as he sat back in the chair. I looked up at him briefly but then quickly dropped my eyes back to my pillow. All the anger had seeped out of me. I had no fight left. I felt ashamed but still very trapped.

"So what happened?"

"I told you," I managed to whisper.

"You didn't tell me why."

I had nothing to say. I didn't know what he wanted to hear. So I said nothing. He sat there for what seemed like forever before he cleared his throat.

"Are you not going to talk?"

"I don't have anything to say," I choked out.

"Well, then I have a few things to say. I am still very shocked that you did what you did. I am also worried that there are other things going on that I still don't know about. Things cannot continue this way. You are sixteen years old, and I understand that I cannot make all your choices for you. But you're also showing me that your choices have not been good ones lately. You are not talking to anyone. You seem angry and depressed. We are all very worried about you."

He paused for a moment, but I kept my eyes on my pillow. "I feel like we have a couple of options at this point, and I'm willing to discuss them with you. First, you could agree to see a counselor. To be honest, I wish I had forced you to go before this, but now I'm not so sure that's enough. The other option is for me to take you to the hospital where you can talk to somebody and see if they think that maybe you should spend a little while in the hospital. I'm feeling that maybe that's what we should do. They can help decide if you need something that drastic."

I felt panic coming back as I realized that my dad wanted to put me in a hospital.

"A hospital for crazy people?" I asked, horrified.

"Not crazy. Just kids who need some help getting through something. I think you need some help. You won't talk to anybody around here; maybe someone there could help you start talking about what's bothering you. If they think you would be fine just seeing a counselor, then that's fine. But I think I'd like to know what they think about the situation."

"Sounds like you already know what you want to do," I said icily. "I just didn't know you thought I was crazy."

"Not crazy, Beka. There is absolutely nothing wrong with needing some help. Most kids who go to psychiatric hospitals just need some help. They know how to help people who are angry and depressed."

"So you think I'm angry and depressed?"

"Yes, that's what it seems like, but since you won't talk about anything, all I can do is assume."

He waited several minutes for me to respond, but when I didn't, he stood up. "Well, I'm going to call the hospital and see if we can go over there this evening and talk to somebody. I'd like you to pack a bag, just in case they think you should stay there. I'll send someone up to get you for meals, but other than that you can stay upstairs until it's time to go." He reached over and hugged me really tight. I stiffened at his touch. I was terrified about even just going over there. I was hurt, too, knowing that my dad thought I was crazy enough to go.

I rummaged through my drawers and threw some clothes into a bag, but then unpacked it and shoved the bag under my bed. I wasn't going to make it easier to throw me out of the house.

I spent the next several hours moving between mild fear and utter panic. Three times I went to the bathroom to see what kind of pills were in the medicine cabinet. I still thought it could be an option. I didn't know whether aspirin would do much to me, but I figured if I took enough of it, maybe it would do the job. I took the bottle of aspirin to my room and counted how many pills there were. Fifty-eight tiny white pills were spread on my blue spread. I stared at them for a while, wondering. It would solve everything, wouldn't it? It would be like disappearing.

I went back to the bathroom and got a glass of water. I took a handful of the pills and held them in my hand. But I couldn't get past the idea that it was wrong, that it could actually doom me for eternity. As long as I was alive there was a chance that things might get better. Then I thought of how slim that chance seemed now. I still couldn't take them. I gathered them up and took them back to the bathroom. I slammed the medicine cabinet door. I felt like a coward. One more thing I failed to do.

Maybe I could work up the courage. But I wasn't sure which would take more courage—to die . . . or to live.

I decided I had better call Gretchen to let her know I wouldn't be coming to her house that night. I was mad at her for stranding me at Jeremy's and not helping me that morning, but I didn't want her to be mad at me. I didn't tell her why except that I got in trouble for being out all night. She thought my dad was being ridiculous, but I didn't respond. I told her I'd call her later. I wondered when I would get around to calling her back.

Anna came and got me for dinner a little while later. It was a very quiet dinner. None of the usual chitchat, and everyone kept looking at me as if I were some kind of bomb that could explode at any moment. After dinner was over, my dad asked me to go get my bag because he had made an appointment with someone at the hospital.

"I don't want to go," I said, not moving from the table. I moved my fork around the rice that was left on my plate.

"Look, Beka, we agreed that we would just go talk to them."

"I didn't agree to anything," I snapped. "You're the one that thinks I'm nuts." I became aware that the others had stopped moving around the kitchen and everyone was now staring at Dad and me. Anna went over and stood behind Lucy, looking scared. But I couldn't back down. I was really scared to go.

"Beka, I want you to get your bag and get in the car," he said firmly.

"No. I'm not crazy. I don't need to go there."

"I never said you were crazy. We are just going to talk to them to see what they think."

"What are you going to do if they think I should stay?"

"Then I'm going to think you should stay."

"I'm not crazy," I repeated.

"Beka, please don't push me on this. We are going to go," he said firmly.

I didn't know what to do. I wasn't sure what he would do if I kept pushing, and I was probably just making things worse anyway. So I pushed back from the table and stomped up the stairs. I heard my dad following me. He stood in my doorway as I packed my bag again. I took as long as I could, but he just stood there watching me. We left without speaking another word to each other.

*　　*　　*

The psychiatric hospital was a separate building across the street from the main hospital. It was a one-level brick building with cushy furniture in the foyer and a large desk by the door. My dad told them who we were, and a receptionist asked us to have a seat while she located the doctor. I fidgeted with the handle on my bag to try to keep my mind off the panic inside of me. After about five minutes a tall man with a bushy black beard came from a door behind the desk. He headed straight for my dad.

"You must be Mr. Madison. Nice to meet you," he said warmly as my dad rose from his chair to shake hands. "I'm Dr. Gayle, and you must be Rebekah. Your father and I spoke briefly this afternoon."

"Thank you so much for seeing us," my father said.

"Oh, not a problem, not a problem," he smiled. "Actually, you would usually have to talk to a few other people before you got to me, but it's Saturday night," he said with a laugh, "and I'm what you get. Well, come with me; let's find a place where we can talk."

We followed Dr. Gayle down several hallways and a couple of locked doors that he opened with a key attached to his belt. He led us to a small room with windows, several chairs, and a table. He carried with him a large notepad, and when we got settled in the room, he pulled out a file folder from his briefcase.

"Well," Dr. Gayle said as he glanced at some notes on his pad of paper, "I always want to get started by telling the kids what this place is all about. They're usually a bit nervous when they come here, and I'd like you to be more relaxed so we can talk. We have a unit here that is only for adolescents.

"Our kids come here usually for one of three reasons: Either they are a danger to themselves, a danger to others, or some aspect of their life has suddenly gone down the tubes. If we decide together tonight that you should stay here, you would have a room on the unit and you would participate in groups with kids your age and talk to a counselor and a doctor individually each day. You would have to remain on the unit and your phone calls are strictly limited, with no contact the first twenty-four hours. You also cannot have any visitors except for immediate family. That means no contact with friends.

Usually, our kids are here anywhere from three days to two weeks. That all depends on you. So, now you know about us. Do you have any other questions?"

I shook my head. It did help to hear exactly what this place was like. It didn't sound as horrible as I had imagined. But I still didn't think I was going to have to stay.

"So, then, why don't you tell me why you're here?" Dr. Gayle asked.

I sat silently. I didn't know what to say. He was nice enough, but I didn't want to talk in front of my father. So I shrugged and kept my eyes on the floor.

"This is part of the problem," my father said as he slumped back in his chair looking defeated.

Dr. Gayle smiled but didn't respond to my father. Unfortunately he stayed focused on me. "Your dad tells me you've been doing some things that aren't typical for you." He paused. "Like staying out all night? Not communicating with anybody? Sound familiar?"

"I guess," I finally muttered.

"Do you ever feel like hurting somebody else?" I shook my head but said nothing. "Do you ever feel like hurting yourself?"

I stiffened as I heard the question. I couldn't be honest about that, but I couldn't seem to deny it either. I didn't move.

Dr. Gayle seemed to have taken my lack of response for a yes, because his next question startled me.

"Do you have a plan as to how you might try to hurt yourself?" I looked up quickly, shocked that he would ask me that. But once again, I didn't know whether to just admit it or try to deny it. I wanted to look at my dad to see what he was thinking, but I was terrified to look over there. *How did he know? How could he possibly know what I had planned to do?*

"Well, your dad tells me that things have gone downhill for you at home and your grades have slipped this semester."

"They're not that bad," I said defensively.

"But they're not your normal grades, am I right?" He continued after a moment. "Well, based on what your dad has already told me, and from what I'm seeing from you, I'd like to suggest that you stay here with us for a few days and see if we can't help you with whatever is bothering you."

The next few minutes were a blur. I heard what he said, but I couldn't believe he really thought I should stay. Had I done anything that crazy or bad? It had all happened so fast. I couldn't stop the tears from dripping down my face as Dr. Gayle talked with my father. I couldn't even follow what they were saying. Then suddenly, Dr. Gayle stood up and shook my dad's hand.

"I'll give you a call tomorrow. She'll be fine with us. We'll take good care of her."

My father grabbed me in a tight hug, and when he pulled back after a few moments, I saw the tears lingering in his eyes. Dr. Gayle put his hand on my back and led me out of the room, down several more hallways and through locked doors.

"This is the adolescent unit," he said as we entered a set of double locked doors. There was a desk that stretched from the doors all the way into a large open area. A tall, dark-haired woman came from behind the desk. She was dressed in regular clothes, but a nametag hung from her shirt. Dr. Gayle spoke with her for a few minutes.

"Harriet will take care of everything you need. We have a group session in about forty-five minutes. I'll see you there." He waved and disappeared down the hallway. Harriet smiled and extended her hand. I shook it but kept my eyes on the floor.

"Well," she said cheerfully. "Let's get you settled in. This is the common area," she said, pointing to the sofas, tables, and chairs in the large open area. "For the first twenty-four hours you are here, you will have to remain in sight of a staff person while you are awake, so you will be spending some time in here tomorrow. Let's go get you settled in."

**By the time** I slumped into the chair in the group room, I felt like I had been through the Inquisition. Harriet and another staff person searched my bags, searched me, and took away anything they felt was a "sharp." In other words, anything I could use to hurt myself. I felt humiliated even though they explained it wasn't just because of me but to keep the other kids safe too. They asked a zillion questions. I had barely thrown my stuff on the bed in my room when another staff person came knocking on the door to tell me it was time for group. She waited for me to follow her, and she led me to a room at the end of the long hallway and motioned for me to go inside. Then she left to go knock on some other doors.

I surveyed the other kids in the room. There were three other girls and four boys. They all looked less than thrilled to be there. Nobody said a word until yet another staff person walked in with the girl who had come to get me from my room. They settled into two of the chairs and waited. We all shifted nervously. After a few minutes, the door opened and Harriet walked in with another girl.

"Sit, Samantha," she ordered. Samantha sat, but she looked really mad.

"I hate these things."

"You only hate them because you never listen," Harriet responded in a cool, even voice. She closed the door as she left, and the attention shifted back to the other two staff.

"I'm Renee and this is Kathy, for the couple of you who may not know us. We seem to have only two more since we were here last night," the younger one observed as she scanned the room.

"Then make the new kids start," a redheaded boy called from the corner where he was rocking back and forth on his chair.

"Maybe we should start with you, Jason. How'd your visit go today with your family?" she countered.

"Well, I would answer that, except that you don't let us swear, and those are about the only words I would like to use," he said bitingly.

"We would just like you to express your feelings in more socially acceptable terms, instead of being pro-fane," Kathy added.

"Oh, I'll start," a really small girl with dark hair volunteered. "Dr. Rudolph said I may be able to go home in a couple of days. As long as I keep eating."

"Great, Katie. Do you think you'll be able to do that?" Renee asked.

She shrugged, "Maybe. I don't know. I just really want to be home for Christmas."

"But you have to keep eating, even when you do get home," another girl with dark hair offered.

"Lisa's right. It's not just about getting out of here. Are you going to be able to stay healthy even after you go home?" Renee pushed.

"I don't know," she said quietly. "I'd like to think I can. Things are better with my mom, so maybe I'll be able to talk to her when I'm feeling bad."

"Well, let's go around the room and make introductions before we go any further. Say your name, your age, and why you're here. Randy, you start." Kathy shifted the focus away from Katie. A few people groaned as if they had to do this a lot.

"Randy, seventeen, I don't like my stepfather," Randy snarled.

"Simon, fifteen, I'm depressed," a thin boy with glasses said quietly. Randy laughed and Kathy shot him a look that shut him up quickly.

"Katie, sixteen, I have trouble eating," Katie said next. "I'm anorexic," she added when Kathy raised her eyebrows at her.

"Lisa, sixteen, I ran away from home. But I'm going home tomorrow," she smiled broadly.

"Beka," I said quietly. "I'm sixteen. I don't know why I'm here. My dad brought me here."

"Jason, seventeen, my teachers don't like my style," Jason sighed.

"Your style?" Renee asked.

"Fine, they don't like me throwing things at them," he sighed.

"Samantha, fifteen, my parents are nuts." Renee and Kathy looked at her, but she refused to say more.

"Brittany, fifteen, I hurt myself," a tall blonde said without emotion. I wondered what she had done, but nobody pushed her to elaborate.

"Greg, twelve, I fight with my mom," the last guy in the circle said loudly.

The rest of the time was more of the same. Kathy and Renee seemed really smart and had some good things to say to everybody, as did some of the kids. They didn't ask me any more questions, and I didn't offer anything. Simon, the depressed boy with glasses, didn't say anything either, but I did learn that he had just gotten there that morning. I assumed that they were just letting us get used to our surroundings.

The meeting ended by nine, and we were all supposed to go to our room and write a letter to someone, anyone we chose. I had to take my paper to the common area and sit at a table in there. The staff people stayed behind the desk and didn't bother me, but I felt like a goldfish being stared at. I looked carefully at the blank paper. I wasn't sure if anyone else was going to see the letter, so it made it harder to decide whom to write. I wanted to write a letter to Mark, but I was too embarrassed to. I was still staring at the paper on the table when Kathy told me it was time to put the lights out and go to bed.

I felt strangely numb as I lay there. The moonlight streamed in from the window across the room, making the room glow eerily. Besides the bed, there was a small dresser, wooden desk, and chair. The room had curtains and wallpaper, but even with them it was still stark and cold. I didn't feel sad or angry anymore. I felt nothing. Like I was in another dimension and it wasn't really me lying there. Every so often, my door would open and someone would look in. It seemed to take forever to fall asleep.

The next morning, I had to stay on the unit to eat breakfast along with Simon, Jason, and Samantha. Everyone else went to the dining room. Samantha told me that we had to stay on the unit until we earned enough points to earn privileges like that. Since it was Sunday, we didn't have any groups until that afternoon. I had to stay in the common area all day, and I was flipping through a magazine when a staff person took me to see the doctor. I had hoped it would be Dr. Gayle, but a tall, thin man with glasses stood up and extended his hand when I walked in.

"Hi, Rebekah, I'm Dr. Rudolph. You'll be seeing both Dr. Gayle and me while you stay here." He flipped through a chart while I sat down in the chair in the small office.

"Do you have any questions for me?" he asked as he put the chart down and took out a notebook and pen and sat back in his chair.

"How long do I have to be here?"

"That's up to you. When you go home we want things to be different for you. Whatever that takes to happen, we'd like it to happen before you leave."

"I don't even know why I'm here. Lots of kids have problems at home and get in trouble. Why am I stuck here?" I was irritated and I let it show in my voice.

"But you hadn't any difficulties until recently. We get especially concerned when things suddenly start going bad." He paused for a moment. "Why don't you tell me about your mom."

"She's dead," I said blankly.

"I realize that. Tell me about her."

I stared blankly at him. And that's pretty much the way the whole time went. He'd ask a question and I'd stare at him. Later, at group, it was more of the same. I got asked several questions, but I'd just shrug or not say anything. By dinnertime, I had crawled into a shell and wouldn't budge. I wasn't even sure why. I knew that they were there to help me, but I didn't know how to open up about all the junk that was inside of me. I felt like as long as I didn't admit it was there, maybe it wasn't. I was sitting in the common area after dinner flipping through the channels on the television when Renee came and sat down beside me.

"So, how's it going?" she asked.

I shrugged and kept flipping.

"I heard you weren't talking. You know, everybody here is here to help you, but we can't help you if you don't talk about what's going on. The faster you deal with it, the faster you will get out of here."

"So I have to talk to get out of here?" I asked before I could stop myself.

"Well, you need to deal with whatever it is that you don't want to deal with. So, in a way, yes, you'll need to talk to make any progress."

"It's too complicated," I sighed, but I could feel myself weakening. Renee seemed sincere and nice. And I didn't want to be stuck there forever. I began to think that if I opened up a little bit with her, it would make things easier. Besides, she didn't know my family, and I wouldn't have to see her after I was able to leave.

"Well, it always seems more complicated when you're stuck in the middle of something. Besides, I have to work till 7 A.M.; we have all the time in the world." She sat back in her chair and waited expectantly.

So I told her. About my mom, the whole Christian thing, the problems with my family, school. Once I started talking, I didn't stop until I had finished everything. Renee didn't say much as I talked; she just nodded every once in a while. As I was talking, I realized the whole story didn't sound that bad. I didn't know how things had gotten so messed up.

"I just don't know how to make things better at home. I feel like a total alien, and I haven't exactly endeared myself to my father lately anyway. He's pretty mad about me staying out all night," I finished. I didn't know what else to tell her.

"He might have been upset, but I think he was mostly worried. That's why you're here. Your family is concerned about you because they love you."

"I don't know why. I haven't been very nice to anyone lately."

"Love isn't about what you do or don't do. It's about who you are. They love you because you're their daughter and sister. Your actions aren't going to change that."

"But I haven't been honest about who I am for years. They'll hate me if they ever find out."

"But don't you see that isolating yourself and not being honest about it is hurting you? Beka, you said you don't even feel like living anymore. That's a pretty serious thing. It's very easy to feel hopeless when we are in something all by ourselves. When we invite other people in to help us, it spreads out the burden, and things don't seem as awful anymore."

I shook my head, "I can't tell them."

"Why not? What's the worst thing that can happen?"

"They'll hate me."

"You already think that anyway."

"It would just be too humiliating."

"So you're too embarrassed to tell them?"

I shrugged.

"Everybody does things that they regret, Beka. Making a mistake and admitting it shows courage. Look, let me share something with you. I'm a born-again Christian just like your family. I believe in God, but I also believe we have an enemy. I think the Enemy has been lying to you for years. Telling you that there is no way out. That you can't tell anyone. His plan is to isolate and destroy you. And he almost succeeded. If your dad hadn't taken such drastic measures, he might have convinced you to take those fifty-eight pills. But it's all a lie. Things won't get worse if you tell them; they'll get better. It won't solve everything, but it will certainly put you on the right path. It's like that first step. You have to take that first step, and then, if you want Him to, God can help you with the rest of it."

This time I shook my head emphatically, "There is no way God would help me with anything. I'm sure that God can't stand the sight of me."

"God does love you. He's been trying to show you that. Nothing is so bad that He would stop loving you. Do you think it's an accident that I was here when you were ready to talk? That I'm a Christian who can really understand what it is that's going on? You have to stop listening to the Enemy. It's important that you start talking and keep talking until you don't feel trapped anymore. You'll have to face your family sooner or later. You can't stay in hiding forever."

I couldn't stop the tears from sliding down my cheeks. I knew that she was right, but it was so much easier to want to escape rather than deal with anything. I looked at Renee. I believed her, but I just didn't know if I had the courage.

"Look, I don't work again until Tuesday evening. That is visitation night. Is your dad coming?"

"I don't know. I guess if I want him to he will. I haven't talked to him."

"Well, your twenty-four hours was up today, so you should be able to make a phone call tomorrow. Call him. Tell him you'd like him to come visit. Visiting starts at 7 P.M. If you want, I can sit with you when you talk to him. You don't have to decide now. In the meantime, tell your story to the others. We missed group tonight, but you'll have several groups tomorrow as well as a session with Dr. Gayle or Dr. Rudolph. Practice talking. Get some ideas. Just realize that some people may not understand the Christian side of things. They're not going to see what the Enemy is doing. But you'll have to talk about it here so that you can go home. The practice will help. I think you haven't talked about things for so long you've nearly forgotten how." She smiled sympathetically.

It was past lights-out by the time we finished, so we said good-bye and I headed to my room. She would be gone by the time I got up in the morning. I lay in bed replaying the conversation in my head. I was already trying to talk myself out of believing her. By the time I walked out to breakfast, I wanted to just stay silent. It was easier. But the thought kept coming to me that I'd never get out of this place if I didn't say something. During breakfast, while the others ate, I thought about making something up. Maybe that would work.

I fought with myself all morning. Then, around ten, they came to get me to see the doctor. I still hadn't decided what to do, and I felt like I was being pushed into cold water before I was ready to jump. As someone walked me to the office, I tried desperately to decide what to do.

"**Good morning,** Beka," Dr. Gayle said warmly as I walked into his office.

As soon as I saw that it was Dr. Gayle, I felt better. Maybe I could do it after all. I had told Renee—one more person wouldn't be such a big deal, would it?

"So," he began as he finished flipping through the notebook on his desk. "You haven't said much in your groups since you've been here. And you didn't want to talk to Dr. Rudolph. Let me explain again how it works here. We want to help you get out of whatever difficulty you're in, but we can't help unless we know what's going on."

"I understand," I said quietly.

"Then what's troubling you, Beka? Why are you so sad?"

He spoke so kindly that the tears began before I could even start speaking. I told him. I started with the Christian thing and went straight through to Friday night. He sat back and just listened. When I had finished, I breathed a long, slow sigh. I felt better. Dr. Gayle had more power than Renee did in this place. Now that I had told him, I began thinking I would be able to go home soon. Maybe I wouldn't even have to stay tonight. Then I began hoping that maybe he wouldn't even suggest telling my dad. He finished writing in his notebook, looked up, and smiled gently.

"It's been pretty scary for you, hasn't it? Feeling so alone and so trapped?"

"Yeah, it was like a snowball rolling downhill. It kept getting bigger and going faster, and I couldn't stop it once it started."

"I wonder. After your mother died, did it feel like you would never be able to fix things because you couldn't fix things with her?"

I nodded, but I couldn't speak as I started crying again.

"It's not true, you know. Things can still be made right with your dad. And even though your mom isn't here, there are ways to help."

"How?" I asked.

"Well, you could write a letter to her, explaining what happened. You won't get a response, of course, but it's a way to deal with those feelings that you have trapped inside of you. And, after you talk to your dad, you may even find out some things that surprise you."

"What do you mean?"

"You said yourself how close your family was. When you begin talking to them about everything, you will probably find out things about your mom that you never knew before."

I had never considered that before. It was an interesting thought. But at the same time, my heart sank, realizing that he wanted me to talk to Dad too.

"Why don't you go ahead and write your mom a letter today," he continued after a moment. "Then maybe you could broach things with your father during your visit tomorrow night."

"Are you going to tell him what I told you today?"

"No, I think that's your job."

"I don't know if I can."

"You told me."

"Yeah, but it doesn't matter if you hate me or think that I'm an awful person. It does matter if my dad thinks that."

"Why would he think you're awful? Nothing you've done or said is as awful as it seems."

We talked a bit more, but he never stopped saying that I needed to talk to my dad. Later, during group time, one of the nurses must have been told that I talked about what was going on, because she kept pressing me to talk in group. I finally did, leaving out some parts of it. Everybody said the same thing, that I should talk to my dad and that it wasn't as bad as it seemed. I was frustrated because they didn't seem to realize how hard it was for me to even think about telling my dad. Every time I began thinking about it, I would just blank out in total fear. I couldn't quite put my finger on why I was so scared. What I had told Dr. Gayle was true, that I didn't want Dad to think of me as an awful person. But it was more than that. I didn't want to disappoint him. Until the last couple weeks, I had always done what was expected, always been the "good girl." When he found out it had all been an act, how would he ever trust me again?

I did call him that evening. He was very anxious to know that I was okay. I assured him I was fine and asked him if he could come the next night. He eagerly agreed and wanted to talk more, but I really wanted to get off the phone. So, we said good-bye, and I hung up feeling like a dark cloud was hanging over my head. I had asked him to come, and I knew I would somehow have to get through that visit.

Later, I once again sat in front of a blank piece of paper. I was crying even before I began to write, thinking about how she would never see the letter anyway, and about how much I really missed her. She had been so beautiful. It felt good to cry, and I didn't try to stop the tears. Slowly, the words began to come.

Dear Mom,

I wish I had had the courage to tell you this a long time ago. But I didn't. And I am so ashamed of what I have done. That night in my room when I told you I wanted to pray, I said it because I thought that was what I had to do to be a part of the family. I didn't really pray anything, but I let you believe I did.

I let everybody believe that I had made a commitment to God. I did everything that I thought I was supposed to, but it had nothing to do with God. It had to do with me wanting to fit in. I felt like I didn't fit in anymore and that everybody else was part of this secret society. So I pretended to join.

I know how wrong it was. And lying about it has made things even worse, and I feel like even more of an outsider than I ever did. I wish I could tell you how sorry I was. I wish I could make things right. I always loved you, but I didn't want you to find out, so I kept my distance. I know that hurt you too. I am so sorry for being so horrible, for lying to you, for not being the daughter you deserved to have. I love you, Mom, and I miss you so much. Please don't hate me for what I've done. I really am so sorry.

Love,
Beka

I folded the letter and slid it into my notebook. I climbed into bed and fell asleep faster than I had in months.

*   *   *

The police officers stand at the door, looking uncomfortable. And Pastor Bandry is there. That can't be good. Dad leads them into the family room, where they perch on the sofa. Lucy hovers near the doorway with Paul at her side. Anna is sleeping. No one wants to wake her.

"I'm so sorry," Pastor Bandry begins. "Greg, she didn't make it."

My father sucks in his breath and holds it, tears spilling from his eyes. He looks at each of us quickly and then blows out his breath and collapses on the floor. Paul wraps his arms around Lucy, and I see her shoulders heave with the sobs muffled in his shirt. Paul's face is pinched and his eyes frantic as he too cries. Pastor Bandry comes to my father and the police officers shifts uncomfortably.

I can't move.

I can't breathe.

She is gone.

*　　　*　　　*

I worried the whole next day about talking to my family. In group, everybody reassured me that it would be fine and that it would be better once I got it over with. Renee came in around 6:30 and sat with me in the common area until Dad arrived. She didn't say anything, which was good. I was too nervous to talk.

They let all the parents in at seven. I saw my father, tall and handsome, come in with an anxious look on his face. He looked around and then caught my eye. He strode toward me and squeezed me in a tight hug.

"Why don't we go to your room, Beka, so we can have some privacy?" Renee suggested.

My dad followed us to my room, and once there he pulled the chair from my desk. Renee went and sat on the windowsill on the other side of the room, and I sat on my bed.

"Mr. Madison, my name is Renee, and I am just here for moral support. Beka needs to talk to you and needed some support to do so. But I'm not going to interfere in your conversation, and Beka, if you feel like you can handle it on your own, just let me know and I'll leave."

My dad nodded and then looked at me expectantly. I closed my eyes, trying to summon the courage to speak. Then, with my eyes still closed, I began to tell him the whole story. With him, I focused more on the Christian/family part of it and just skimmed over the junk at school and the Mark situation. He tried to protest a few times, but he stopped when I told him I just needed to get the whole thing out.

By the time I had finished, we were both crying and he was on my bed next to me with his arm around me. I was too ashamed to look up, but once I stopped talking, he simply grabbed me and held me tight and whispered, "I love you" over and over in my ear. For the first time, I was able to hug him back. I didn't want him to let me go. I don't know how long we stayed like that or how long I cried, but by the time we sat back from each other, I felt a huge relief. I knew it wasn't all over, but I felt like the worst of it was.

"Beka, can I respond to a few things you said? If you're not ready, just tell me."

"No, it's okay," I said as I wiped the tears away. "I just needed to get it over with. I was so scared to tell you."

"Why? Why, honey?"

"I thought you'd hate me. That you'd be disappointed in me."

"Sweetheart, nothing you do is going to change how much I love you. We have some stuff to work through, but we'll get through it together. You don't have to be alone anymore." We hugged again, and then he sat back seriously. "Is that everything? Is that everything that's been bothering you?"

"Pretty much. There's some stuff at school, but it's really not that important. Just confusing."

"Well, I don't want to skip over that, because you were with school friends Friday night. I'm still concerned about that, but we can work on that later. But right now I want to talk to you about your mom."

"Do you think she would hate me?"

"Never, not in a million years. But, Beka, we've known for quite some time that you weren't living life as a true Christian. We can never know someone's heart, but we did wonder how sincere you were the night you got saved or didn't get saved. We suspected that you did it for reasons other than a real encounter with God. But we weren't sure, and we weren't about to squelch you. So we waited and watched.

"Your mom and I actually talked about it quite a bit. We didn't confront you on it later because we were hoping you *would* have an encounter with God that would help you get on the right track. Looking back, I guess we should have talked to you about it. But we didn't want you to feel accused or isolate you even more. We weren't sure what to do. We prayed about it a lot, but maybe we should have talked to you, asked you about it. Then your mom died and I mistakenly thought that all of our recent problems were because of your mom's death. I didn't know that your turmoil went all the way back to that night."

"You knew?" was all I could muster.

"Suspected. We weren't sure. Why, are you surprised?"

"I thought you'd be shocked and horrified."

"No, I'm not surprised. It all makes sense to me now, actually. I can see how you felt so alone, and I can imagine how scary it's been. I do wish you had told me sooner."

"Now I wish I had too."

"As far as your relationship with God goes, that has to be your decision. I'm sorry you felt pressured about it before. Nobody meant to pressure you. And you don't have to be saved to be part of our family. I want that for you, but I can't make it happen. Everybody has to choose whether they follow God or not."

"But you all have God in common, and I just can't seem to find my way. I can't connect with it. I don't know what's wrong with me."

"Nothing is wrong with you, darling. You weren't ready, that's all. God draws each of us in different ways and at different times. Do you even understand what salvation is all about?"

"Not really. I mean, I know all the words, but I'm not sure what they all mean."

"Do you want to understand it?"

"I think I want to find out. But not tonight. Maybe not even tomorrow. But I want to maybe try to understand what it's all about."

"What? What's that look? Why did your face just fall?"

"It's just that, well, I guess I'm going to have to tell everyone else about this too."

"We do need to tell your brother and sisters. But I'll be there with you. You won't be alone."

"Do you think I could come home?"

"Do you feel like you're ready?"

I nodded.

"Well, let me go talk to someone and see what I can do." He hugged me again and then left the room. It wasn't until that moment that I realized that Renee wasn't there anymore. I walked down the hallway and saw her sitting in the common area with Katie. She smiled when she saw me.

"How'd it go?"

"Fine. Why did you leave?"

"It looked like things were going fine. I figured once you got started you'd make it. It didn't go as bad as you thought, did it?"

"No. Actually, he wasn't even surprised."

"I thought that might be the case. It's actually pretty easy sometimes to tell the difference between someone who is really saved and walking with God and someone who isn't."

"Well, he's checking to see if I can go home. There doesn't seem to be any reason to stay."

"You don't feel like hurting yourself anymore, do you?"

"No. I'm not sure I would have ever really done anything like that anyway. I just felt trapped and I didn't think there was any way to escape. I don't feel trapped anymore. I actually feel pretty free for the first time in years. I don't have any secrets anymore."

"The truth always sets us free. That's true whether you're a Christian or not."

"Beka," I heard my dad's voice behind me. "Honey,

they don't want to let you leave tonight. They want you to see Dr. Gayle in the morning, and then if that goes fine, I can come get you by lunchtime. I'm sorry. That's the best I could do."

"It's okay. I'll be fine."

"Okay, well, they're telling me that I have to go. Tell them to call me at work and I'll come get you as soon as they'll let me."

We hugged and said good-bye. It felt good to smile and hug him. To not feel like I had to be stiff and distant. I was glad to be going home. Just a few more people to tell and it would all be over.

Well, maybe not over, but certainly better. Wednesday night after dinner, Dad brought everybody into the family room and helped me tell them what had been going on. I felt really awkward, even though my dad was supportive and encouraging. I apologized, but I felt like it sounded pitiful compared to what I had done.

"Does this mean you feel better, Beka?" Anna asked from her spot on the floor.

"Yeah, Anna, I do feel better." I smiled at her. She leaped off the floor and came and crawled on my lap.

"Does it mean you don't believe in God anymore?" Anna asked, obviously a bit confused.

"Well, I'm not sure how I feel about God right now," I answered her. "But I'm going to try and figure that out."

She seemed satisfied with that response. I snuck a look at Paul, who hadn't said anything since dinner.

"Paul," I began cautiously, "I know I've been rotten. I think I probably took it out on you worst of all. I really am sorry."

"I forgive you. And I'm really glad it's all out in the open. But I have to admit, I really hope you get things sorted out with God too."

"I know, but please don't pressure me," I said quietly.

"Paul," Dad interceded, "Beka needs to be able to make her own decision." He turned his head to speak to everybody. "That goes for everybody. If you're worried, then you can pray about it or talk to me about it. But we have to trust God that He will help Beka find her way. In the meantime, let's make sure we give her lots of time, love, and space to figure things out, okay?"

Everybody nodded and murmured an agreement. I felt better about things, but I also felt a little like I was in a fishbowl. I felt like everyone would be watching my every move. Plus, I had said more than once that I would try to figure things out with God, and I didn't even know where to begin. It felt pathetic that I had been going to church for years and yet I had no idea what to do. It all seemed too complicated, and I had stopped listening to everybody so long ago that God had become a jumble of three-syllable words in my head: salvation, righteousness, justified. Not to mention what I had done already. I had lied to my family, but I had also lied to God. Would He even want anything to do with me?

I was so preoccupied with trying to spend some time with my family and let them see that I was trying that I had nearly forgotten about school. Apparently, both Lori and Gretchen had called while I was in the hospital, but fortunately my family told them that I was away, but they weren't more specific. I certainly didn't want Gretchen to know where I had been, but I thought about telling Lori. After all, she had trusted me with her secret.

I decided to just call Lori back. I would have to deal with Gretchen later.

"Merry Christmas," a cheerful voice called into the phone.

"Merry Christmas," I returned. "Is this Kari Lynn?"

"Yes," she answered.

"Is Lori there? This is Beka."

"I'll get her." I could hear her yelling Lori's name in the background.

"Hi, Beka. I'm so glad you called," Lori said enthusiastically a few moments later.

"Hi. I called to wish you a Merry Christmas. And to see how things are going."

"They're great," she bubbled. "We have a court date in January, and if all goes well, the adoption will become official."

"That's wonderful," I said sincerely. I really was happy for her.

"How are things going for you? Your sister said you were away. Where'd you go?"

"Umm, well, actually, I was in the hospital. The psychiatric hospital, not the regular hospital," I added when I heard her gasp.

"Oh, my. What happened? If you don't want to tell me, that's fine," she added quickly.

I told her about the weekend before and staying out all night and how I ended up going to the center. But as I was telling her, I began relating the whole story. She listened quietly. When I was finished, I realized how much I had opened myself up.

"Please don't tell anyone," I begged. "Everybody who needs to know knows."

"Sure, Beka. I wouldn't say anything. Have I told you that the Rollinses are born-again Christians too?"

"No. Are they really? I mean, it doesn't surprise me. They're really nice."

"Yeah. I've been to church with them and all that. And they've told me about their faith, but they haven't said a whole lot else. I guess they don't want to pressure me. Or maybe they're waiting for me to ask more. I really hadn't given the whole thing much thought, but after hearing your story, maybe I should find out more. You know," she said carefully, "we could find out together if you want. I mean, we could talk to Megan and we could ask her questions. That might be easier for you than asking your family or people at your church about it right now. Besides, I kind of want to know more now too."

"Maybe you're right," I agreed. "I don't quite know where to start anyway. And it is hard to ask my family questions about it. I feel like even my baby sister knows more than I do. Which is slightly embarrassing."

"Look. I'll broach the subject with Megan and maybe we can get together right after Christmas. Speaking of

Christmas, are you doing okay with that? I mean, without your mom and all?"

"You know, so much has been going on that I haven't had much time to dwell on it. I guess I'll find out tomorrow. Do you suppose I had this big crisis now so that I could avoid dealing with it?"

"Maybe." She laughed. "It sounds like you certainly stirred everything up."

We agreed to talk more after Christmas. I was nervous about possibly talking with Megan, but I had to agree it would be easier for me to find out about God that way. I would definitely feel freer to ask questions.

*   *   *

Christmas morning was very different than it had been. Even Anna seemed somber. Everybody came down in their pajamas and gathered in the living room around the Christmas tree. Nobody dove into the presents or stockings, even though it looked like my dad had tried to make everything look really nice.

"How do we do this now?" Lucy asked out loud to nobody in particular.

"Maybe we could each talk about a special memory with Mom. You know, to remember her and let her know she's in our hearts," Paul suggested.

"Do you suppose Mom can see us?" Lucy asked quietly.

"I like to think she can," Dad said sadly. "I don't know how everything works up there in heaven, but heaven is beyond time. The time between when she left and we will leave may have seemed like the blink of an eye to her. I don't know. But I know she's here in spirit."

We went around the room slowly, as everybody shared special things they remembered about Mom. Mostly they chose funny memories, and despite the fact that we had tears just below the surface, we laughed and giggled. I felt closer to my family than I had in years. Even I was able to share about the time that Mom had taken me out to dinner and I had knocked the candle over on the table and set the tablecloth on fire. She put out the fire like a pro, but we both had thought that it was hilarious. The restaurant hadn't found it as amusing as we had.

By the time we finished, the room was more light-hearted and Dad said a prayer to close the time. The rest of the morning was a more typical Christmas. We opened our gifts, read from the gospel of Luke, and even joked around some. We once again got caught up in the excitement and I found myself smiling and enjoying the morning.

I received some sweet gifts from everyone. Lucy had taken a notebook, covered it with fabric, and made a beautiful journal for me that closed with two yellow rib-bons. I was so glad that I always worked on Christmas presents during the summertime. We were supposed to make them, not buy them, so I had always done them over the summer when I had more time. Anna was thrilled with the small jewelry box I had found at a garage sale. I had refinished the outside and then used stencils to draw a horse in a field of flowers. But the best present came later from my dad. I was at the table playing a game with Lucy, Paul, and Anna when Dad came up and handed me three letters.

"Sorry, sweetie, I forgot to give these to you when you got home." He handed them to me and left the room. I flipped through them quickly, recognizing my grandmother's handwriting and my aunt's, but when I got to the third one there was just an address in the top corner and I didn't recognize the handwriting. I opened it carefully, being sure not to tear the address. It was a Christmas card. I sucked in my breath when I saw Mark's name at the bottom. I read slowly, savoring each word.

Dear Beka,

I hope this card finds you happy and healthy this Christmas. I hope you are also enjoying your break. I am looking forward to getting to know you better during our rehearsals next year. Take care.

Mark

It was short, but I was thrilled. Maybe, just maybe. I was almost afraid to hope. I wondered what he would think if he knew I was in the hospital. I didn't even consider telling him.

An even bigger surprise came the next day. I was in my room writing in my journal—a habit I had agreed to begin when I spoke with Dr. Gayle my last day in the hospital. I enjoyed doing it, and it helped me sort my thoughts out a little better. I was actually writing about Mark and contemplating whether I was being realistic or living in a fantasyland over the situation when the phone rang.

It was Mark.

"Hello, Beka?" he questioned politely.

"Yes."

"Hi! This is Mark."

"Hi," I responded, not sure of what to say.

"Did you have a nice Christmas?"

"Yes, actually I did. Did you?" I felt really awkward. I wanted to talk to him, but I felt like the conversation was stiff.

"Yes, thanks for asking. Well, I was kind of calling because I have a proposition for you."

"What is it?" I asked, relieved that he was getting to his point.

"Well, I'm going to host a small New Year's Eve party at my house. No alcohol, of course. It will mostly be some friends of mine who don't go to our school, but I thought you might like to come."

My mind began racing. My first thought was how great it would be to go to Mark's, but he was making it clear that it was mostly going to be people I didn't know. I immediately thought of asking him if I could bring Lori, but that worried me too. Lori was pretty, smart, and nice. If I brought her, would he take an interest in her, breaking my heart? I couldn't decide what to do.

"Don't feel pressured to come," he added when I didn't respond right away. "My friends are really nice though. You might like them."

"Oh, it's not that. I was just wondering if I could bring a friend." I knew I might regret it, but it popped out of my mouth before I could stop it.

"Gretchen and her crowd wouldn't be interested, I

can promise you. I'm sure they'll have their own type of party."

"I wasn't talking about Gretchen. There's a girl at school who's new this year and I've kind of made friends with her. She still doesn't know a lot of people." The more I spoke, the happier I was that I had thought of her. She really would appreciate the offer, even if she wasn't allowed to go. Then I remembered my recent history and wondered if I would even be allowed to go.

"You're more than welcome to invite her. I figured we'd start things around seven. Sound all right?"

"Sure, but I'll have to check with my dad and all that."

"Do you need a ride?"

"I'm not sure," I said but was thrilled that he had offered.

"Okay, well, why don't you just give me a call in the next few days and let me know, all right?"

"Sounds great," I said, probably too enthusiastically. I couldn't believe that I might be able to see him again before school started. And he had invited me when he hadn't invited others from school. Was it too much to hope for?

I sat down with Dad that night and explained about how it was Gretchen that I was with when I went to the beer party and that Lori and Mark were not a bad influence. He raised his eyebrows at that revelation, making the comment that we would discuss Gretchen later. But he did agree to let me go to Mark's New Year's party after I agreed that he was going to call Mark's parents to talk to them about it as well. He said he really wanted to start things fresh and give me a real chance but that he was going to keep better tabs on things for a while. I was glad that he was being so forgiving, but I knew the one thing that was missing from our conversation was how I was doing in my dealings with God. I felt bad for not following through yet, but it wasn't long before I got a chance to make good on my promise of figuring out where I was with God.

Lori called the next morning and said that Megan was really excited to sit down and talk with us and wanted me to come over that very afternoon. I was happy to know that I would at least be able to tell Dad that I was trying, but I was really nervous about it. I was so scared that I would feel pressured to do something about what she said. But I didn't want to go back on my promise to Lori or my own family. So I agreed to come over. I knew my dad would have no problem with it after I explained my reasons why.

"That sounds great, Beka. I'm so glad you found someone you can talk to about the Lord. I know it must be intimidating to talk to us," he said when I told him where I wanted to go.

"Not intimidating exactly. But I guess I would rather talk to someone who doesn't belong to our family at this point."

"Will you let me know how it goes, and how you're feeling about things soon, though? I want to make sure we keep communicating."

I agreed, and a few hours later I was driving my car over to Lori's house. I felt really sick to my stomach and nearly turned around and went home twice, but I kept reminding myself that we were just going to talk to her.

Lori looked a little nervous too when she answered the door and showed me into their living room. Megan was already there and greeted me with a warm hug when I came in.

"I'm so glad you could come over, Beka. I had David take Kari Lynn out this afternoon so we could have some privacy. Oh, don't look so scared," she said, and laughed. "I'm not going to force you to do anything or say anything. I just want to be able to answer your questions and give you the information you need. It's up to you to decide how you feel about it all." She smiled and hugged me again. I felt a little better after that.

"Okay, you two," she started as we settled into the chairs. "I wanted to see if you had any specific questions first or whether you wanted me to just share with you."

I glanced at Lori and she looked at me. We both kind of shrugged. I know I had questions, but I couldn't form them into words.

"Well," she said, "why don't I start, and then if you have a question, just jump in, okay?" We nodded in agreement and relief.

"It's all very simple, really. I'm going to share with you some things that the Bible says about us and about God. The most important thing that you must understand is that God loves you both. The Bible says that He cares about you so much that He even has the very hairs on your head numbered."

"Seriously? That's kind of weird." Lori reached up and pulled her dark hair forward to look at it. Megan grinned for a moment and then leaned forward.

"You both have had some very tragic things happen to you, and it can be very easy to think that God doesn't care about you. But I promise you He does. When you live in a sinful world, full of sinful people, bad things can happen.

"Anyhow, the Bible tells us about a lot of sins we can see, like lying and murder, but it also talks about sins that we can't see, like greed and pride. It also says that if we break even one of God's laws, we've broken them all. So no one can say they aren't a sinner. Since God is perfect and holy, sin keeps us from being able to go to God. It's like He is on one side of a cliff, and we are on the other. The pit between Him and us is our sin. Sin separates us from God." Megan shifted on the couch, took a sip of her coffee, and continued.

"Thankfully, He did not leave us like that. God said that when people sinned there must be a blood sacrifice made to cover the sin. So God sent His Son, Jesus, to live in this world. Jesus was the perfect sacrifice because He never sinned—so His blood could then cover our sins. With our sins covered, we are able to know God the Father and experience who He is. Our sin no longer has to separate us from God because of Jesus' sacrifice. That's what people are talking about when they say 'accepting Jesus.' It means that you not only believe in Him, but that you recognize yourself as a sinner and acknowledge that you need Jesus to be the sacrifice for your sins. That's why people call Him the Savior—He saves us from our sins and from being forever separated from God."

"So that's why the cross is so important? Because it reminds people that Jesus is their Savior?" Lori leaned forward and wrapped her arms around her knees.

"Yes, exactly, it reminds us that we are sinners and that Jesus had to die in our place. When we accept His sacrifice, we are 'saved' from our sins. But being saved is only the beginning. Walking life out as a Christian is a process. We don't stop sinning just because we are Christians. Even those who are saved must continually go to God to ask Him to forgive us of our sins. This is called repenting. We ask Him to forgive us and ask Him to help us turn away, or stop doing, that sin. When we get saved, God gives us the gift of the Holy Spirit. It is the Holy Spirit, who is also part of God, who gently shows us our sin." Megan stopped when she saw me squirm. "What is it, Beka?"

"I don't know. I guess I always found that part confusing. I mean, there's God, there's Jesus, and I'm not sure I ever understood the Holy Spirit part of it all."

Megan smiled. "It can be confusing. It's just important that you understand that the Holy Spirit is God, just as Jesus is God."

I nodded and she went on.

"The Holy Spirit shows us our sin so that we can repent, but He is also there to guide us. This is one of the most exciting parts of being a Christian.

"You see, the Bible says that He has a plan for each of us. Some may use the words 'His will,' but basically it's a plan for our lives. Because He loves us so much and knows so much more than we do, that plan is better than anything we could dream up for ourselves. When we are Christians, God is there to help us make decisions and guide us on the correct path. Once we are saved, we are no longer wandering around in the darkness. We have the Father, Son, and Holy Spirit to guide us and help us become more like Jesus, the perfect person. As Christians, we try to grow and learn more about God each day. We follow Him not because we have to, but because we see our need for Him and how miserably we fail without Him."

That's for sure, I thought. I couldn't help but wonder if maybe I had simply messed up too much. That Jesus had given me my chance and I had blown it. Taking a deep breath, I tried to pay attention as Megan finished up.

"We won't become perfect before we die, but we keep moving towards that goal of becoming like Jesus. Then, when we do die, we will spend all of eternity with God in heaven. No one knows what heaven is really like, but the only way to ultimately get there is through Jesus. Without Jesus in our lives, we are doomed to wander this earth in darkness and then be eternally separated from God after we die." She looked at each of us carefully. "I've said an awful lot. Do you have any questions; is there anything that doesn't make sense?"

I was stunned that everything made as much sense as it did. It was like she took all the puzzle pieces I had seen for years and put them together for me so I could actually see the picture. I had never seen the picture before.

"When did you become a Christian?" Lori asked.

"Back in college," she said and smiled. "I was kind of a mess. I was drinking and partying a lot, headed nowhere. I had always believed in God and I had thought that was enough. I met some girls who began telling me the truth, and eventually I not only understood what they were saying, but I believed it with all my heart. It was hard to turn things around at first because I had to stop partying with my old friends. But God helped me to set my life on a better course."

"I can't see you doing those things," Lori said as she laughed.

"You'd be surprised what people are capable of when they have no direction in their lives. It's easier to get pulled into things." She turned and looked carefully at me. "You seem like you're struggling with something, Beka. What is it?"

It unnerved me that she could see right through me. I debated about whether to open up about my fake conversion. It was a question I had to have answered though. "Well," I said slowly, "I feel like I've already messed things up too much." I told her about my family and my secret. Even though I had told the story many times before, I seemed to cry even more as I told Megan. I felt like God was listening, and I was so ashamed of what I had done. While I was telling Megan what had happened, she moved over next to me and put her arm around me. When I was finished she hugged me tight.

After a few minutes, she took my face in her hands and looked straight into my eyes. "Beka, there is nothing, absolutely nothing that you could ever do to make God stop loving you or keep you from Him if you're truly sorry. I can tell that you are very sorry for what you did. No sin is too great for Christ's blood." She sat back and addressed us both.

"You see, I have told you most of the story, but there is another part of this. This world has only two kingdoms: the kingdom of darkness and the kingdom of light. God is in the kingdom of light, and anyone who is a Christian is there with Him. Anyone who is not saved dwells with Satan in the kingdom of darkness. Satan doesn't want to lose anybody to God, so he will lie to keep you in darkness. His whole purpose on earth is to steal, kill, and destroy. When we live in darkness, it's easier to believe Satan's lies. Beka, he made you believe there was no way out and that God would never accept you now. Those are lies. He wanted you to think you were all alone. But God had other plans. He put all sorts of things in your life to help show you that He loves you.

"The thing to remember is that there are only two choices, two armies to join. Either we are in God's camp or the Enemy's. There are no other choices. Most of the people who are in the Enemy's camp don't even know that it is Satan who influences them. Some even believe if they just try to be a good person, they'll go to heaven and that'll be enough. More lies. That's not the way it works, but that's what Satan does."

"So you really think that God still loves me?" I asked quietly.

"No question about it. He adores you. He got you here, didn't He? It's not an accident that Lori moved in with us, that you all met, and that you are here right now at this very moment."

"What about my mom, though? I can't fix things with her."

"No, not the way we think of as fixing things. But you can fix things with God and trust that she is in God's hands now. You said yourself that your parents kind of knew what had happened. I can almost guarantee that your mom's prayer for you was that you would make a real decision for Christ one day. That would be much more important to her than you apologizing to her personally."

"Do you think my mom and dad are in hell then?" Lori asked suddenly.

"Well," Megan said carefully, "they didn't live their lives like Christians, but we never know for sure what happens in another person's heart before they die. I think there are plenty of people who wait till those last moments to get right with God. Of course, they miss the joy of living life with Him here on earth, but they may be saved in the end. There just isn't a way for us to know for sure this side of eternity."

"Do you have to say something specific to God to get saved? And do you have to have somebody with you?" I asked. I wasn't trying to change the subject, but I didn't want to leave without asking everything I wanted to.

"There are some things you should cover in a prayer to be saved. Basically, you need to admit that you're a sinner, recognize that Jesus is God's Son and that He died to pay for your sin. Then, ask Him to forgive you for your sin and let Him know that you want Him to be in charge of your life.

"But exactly what you say isn't as important as what's in your heart. That's why when you were with your mom that night, you could have even said the words out loud and it wouldn't have made a difference. God knew they weren't coming from your heart. As for having somebody with you, I would say no. You don't have to have somebody with you, but I always recommend it. Because even after you get saved, Satan doesn't stop trying to lie to you. There is something about having someone with you to witness your turning to God that makes things more solid. Then, when Satan tries to tell you that you didn't mean it or God didn't really accept you, there is someone to help you fight those lies."

"I don't need any more convincing," Lori announced. "I didn't know any of this stuff before; I never even went to a church until I moved here. I've watched you all and wondered why you were so kind and so generous. Why you would bother with a sixteen-year-old orphan? You came and said you would take me in, when everyone else said I didn't have a chance. I know God must be real because of who you guys are. I don't want to wait another minute. What do I have to say?" She looked up at Megan expectantly from the floor. Megan had tears dripping down her face, but she was smiling.

"I love you, Lori," she said as she moved onto the floor next to her and hugged her.

"Do you want me to leave?" I asked. I didn't know if Lori wanted it to be private between them.

"No," Lori said emphatically. "I want you to stay. So, what do I have to do?"

Megan asked Lori a couple of questions and then led her in a prayer. There was nothing overly dramatic about it, but when Lori looked up she had a fire in her eyes I had never seen before. She had always been pretty, but there was a new confidence there that I hadn't seen. It startled me.

"What about you, Beka?" Lori asked pointedly.

"Oh, I don't know. Do you mind if I take a walk and think about it all for a few minutes? It's a lot for me to take in."

"Sure, we'll be right here when you get back," Megan smiled.

I put on my coat and went into their backyard. It was pretty big and private. I went and sat on their tire swing. Everything made sense to me now, but something was still stopping me. I felt like I needed something else, but I didn't know what.

I swung slowly, not thinking about anything in particular. After a while, I started saying, "Help me, God. Help me see." I didn't even know what I needed to see, but I figured He did. I decided to stay out there as long as necessary. It was already getting dark, and it was getting colder by the minute.

Then something extraordinary happened.

I looked up at the tree above me, thinking about how bare everything was, and suddenly a large butterfly flew towards me and landed on the branch above my head. I looked at it in shock, knowing that butterflies and winter don't mix. Yet there it was, calmly sitting on the branch, gently moving its wings every couple of moments. As I looked at it, I thought about how they start out as caterpillars and are completely changed into beautiful butterflies. The thought stuck with me. *Was God saying that I could change too?*

I was flooded with such a peace. Now I was sure. I couldn't explain why that little butterfly changed things, but it did. It was like God was reassuring me that it was okay. That I could really change. I went back in the house with a renewed confidence. I knew what they were saying was true, and, for the first time, I felt like it was true for me too. Megan and Lori both prayed with me after we talked for a little bit. Megan wanted to meet with Lori and me after school once a week to make sure we got on the right track with things. I happily agreed. I was thrilled and happy that things were finally right with God, but I wasn't really sure what I was supposed to do from there.

"I almost forgot," I told her as I was leaving. "We were invited to a New Year's Eve party at Mark's house. He's a guy from school, and the party is going to be totally nonalcoholic and his parents will be there. I've met them. They're really nice." I had almost forgotten to mention it. Lori looked at Megan to see what she thought.

Megan shrugged and said, "I'll have to talk to your dad about it tonight and talk with this boy's parents."

"You could call my dad if you want. He's going to call Mark's parents anyway."

"Okay, I'll talk to your dad and then I'll let you know, okay Lori?"

"Sure." She smiled. "I'll call you later, Beka."

*   *   *

Driving home was odd. I felt different. Not drastically different, but different. I felt like a tremendous weight had been lifted off of me. I wasn't sure how to tell my dad. I wondered if maybe he wouldn't even believe me. I really didn't want a big fuss to be made, but I wanted to tell him.

I had to go looking for him when I got home. I finally found him in the basement. He had a workshop down there and he was working on some project with some wood. He didn't see me right away. I watched him sand the wood carefully and methodically. He seemed so strong. While I was watching him though, I thought of how lonely he must be without Mom. They had been so close, so in love. It was the first time I had ever really thought about how much he must miss her. I had been so focused on myself for so long. I felt bad for making things even harder for him.

"Beka, are you okay?" he asked anxiously when he turned and saw me at the bottom of the stairs. He wiped his hands on a cloth and then wiped the tears from my cheek. "What's wrong?"

"I came to tell you I was sorry," I choked out.

"Sorry?"

"For making things so hard around here lately. For doing what I did. For what I put you through."

"Honey, we've already talked about this. I forgive you."

"But you don't understand," I cried. "I'm really sorry. I'm not sure I was sorry enough before. I really see what I did, now."

"Okay, darling. I still forgive you," he said hugging me.

"Daddy, I prayed that prayer today at Lori's house. For real this time. I understand now what it all means. It didn't make sense to me before, but today it did. God sent me a butterfly." He slowly leaned back from hugging me so he could see my face as I was talking to him. "Please forgive me, Daddy," I asked, feeling desperate. "I'm so sorry."

"Honey, calm down," he said soothingly. "I do forgive you. And I know God does too. Now, I want to know what happened. What do you mean a butterfly?"

"There was a butterfly. And it's December. I felt like it was God telling me that I could change too. Just like a butterfly." As I said the words aloud, I suddenly had doubts. "Do you think God sent the butterfly?"

"If it encouraged you and gave you peace, then I have no doubt that God meant that butterfly for you. He talks to us in many ways. Often, when we are first getting to know who He is, He'll give us signs that help us."

"It *did* give me peace." I smiled. I eagerly filled him in on the afternoon and the help that Megan gave me. He was glad that Megan was willing to meet with Lori and me to help us get settled. He did mention that he wanted to talk with her about some things before we started, but that didn't faze me in the least. I couldn't remember the last time I was so happy.

"Oh, I also talked to Mark's parents today, so it's fine for you to go."

"Well, Lori's mom wanted to talk with you about that, so you could bring up the meetings then if you want," I suggested.

He agreed to call Megan, and we talked for a bit

longer. It struck me how odd we must have looked sitting at the bottom of the basement stairs having a conversation that was so important to me. I was so relieved that my father was kind about the whole thing. After months of fighting him and avoiding him, I now wanted to talk to him about everything. Well, almost everything.

I didn't want to mention my feelings for Mark. Partly, I was a little embarrassed that I felt so strongly about someone I really didn't know very well. And deciding to become a Christian kind of threw a new wrench into everything. Was it okay to like boys? I didn't know how it all worked. I *did* want to tell Lori about it before we went to the party. I figured she'd understand.

The days until New Year's Eve passed extremely slowly. Lori was allowed to go, and I worked up my nerve to call Mark and let him know, but he wasn't home. I left a message with his mother and told her that he didn't need to return the call. My dad had helped me fill in my family on my salvation, but I didn't tell them about the butterfly. I felt it was special. I didn't mind my dad knowing, but that was enough. Everybody was enthusiastic for me but somewhat cautious. I couldn't blame them. All I could do was show them that things had changed.

One problem that came up sooner than I had expected was Gabby. My dad told us one night at dinner that we were going out to the farm the next day. I didn't say anything, and I knew it was assumed that I would go, but I was surprised at how much I still didn't want to be around her. Or for her to be around my family. I didn't quite know what to do with it. I decided to not make a fuss about it and try to go with a positive attitude.

That worked for about ten minutes. I started getting irritated almost as soon as we arrived. She was too friendly with my sisters and smiled too much at my father. I didn't even know how to begin working through my anger towards her. Maybe I was just jealous. I decided I would have to talk with Megan about it. She would know what I was supposed to do.

While Anna was riding, I wandered up a small hill and sat beneath a tree. Along with pondering the Gabby situation, I daydreamed about the party. I imagined Mark telling me that he liked me and thought about having a boyfriend for the first time. I didn't know if it was okay to want it or not, but at this point, I wanted it and couldn't do anything about it. I was so deep in thought that I jumped when Lucy came up to me.

"I didn't mean to scare you. Do you want to be alone?"

"No, it's fine. I was just thinking."

"It's awfully cold out. I think Anna would want to ride in a blizzard," she said as she shook her head.

I laughed. "I think you're right."

"You know, I'm really glad that things are better. I didn't know what to say anymore because everything I said seemed wrong."

"I know how you felt. That's the way I was feeling too."

"I wanted to give you something," she said as she took a piece of paper from her coat pocket. She fumbled to open it with her gloves on. "Mom gave this to me at one of our Bible studies. She told me to pass it along to everybody else when it was time. It's a list of Scriptures that were special and meaningful to her. She said it was like sharing a part of her heart with us. I haven't given the list to Anna yet. I figured she meant when she was older. Mom always knew you'd get things straightened out eventually."

I took the page from her with the tears already filling my eyes. I ached for her when I saw her gentle handwriting. The numbers and words meant nothing to me right then, but all of a sudden, I was desperate for a Bible so that I could find them all.

"Thank you, Lucy. And I'm sorry for the times I've been mean to you. I know it will take me a while to get to where everybody else is though, so be patient with me, okay?"

"I know," she said as she reached over and hugged me. "Just remember, though, we are all still learning. We'll all still make mistakes. We just get to handle them differently now."

We left for home soon after that. I gripped the piece of paper Lucy had given to me in my pocket. I couldn't wait to get home and look them up.

I woke up the next morning and immediately got nervous. It was New Year's Eve. And I would see Mark in a mere ten hours. I had stayed up late the night before trying to write out the verses that Mom had written down. Some of them took me a long time to find. I was still only halfway through the list. Not all of the Scriptures made sense to me yet, but one in particular stood out to me. It was Psalm 32:8. It said, "I will instruct you and teach you in the way you should go; I will counsel you and watch over you." I already had so many questions about how God wanted me to handle things that those words were a great comfort to me. God really was going to help me figure it all out. Sooner or later.

I spent the rest of the morning looking up more Scriptures, but the afternoon was reserved for getting ready for the party. Since things were better at home, I had invited Lori to come over after lunch, have dinner, and then spend the night when we got home from the party. She was thrilled, and I wanted to have time to tell her about Mark. I knew I was being selfish though, because part of the reason I wanted to tell her was so she wouldn't take a liking to him too. I figured if she knew how I felt she would keep her distance.

"Your family is great," she said enthusiastically after we had settled down into my room. "Anna and Kari Lynn really are almost like twins!"

"I know. Isn't that weird? You know, I want to talk to you about this party tonight."

"Sure. I'm really excited about going. I haven't been to a party in a long time."

"Well, Mark, the guy who's giving this party, is a little different."

"What do you mean? Does he have two heads? Why do you look so serious?"

"Well . . ." I squirmed. "It's just he's a bit different than the other guys at school."

"You like him, don't you?" She laughed. "That's great. Well, at least I think it's great. Do you suppose it's okay? You know, like what does God say about relationships and stuff at our age?"

"I have no idea," I admitted, relieved that she had the same questions I did. "I know he's very moral; he doesn't drink or swear or smoke or any of that kind of thing. That's good, isn't it?"

"Yeah, I'm sure that's good, but I'm new at this too. Maybe we should call Megan."

"I thought about that. It just seems so common to immediately ask her about boys."

"I think she'll understand. We're sixteen, not sixty."

"Yeah, but it's kind of embarrassing. I mean, I've liked guys before, but I never really told anybody. Besides, maybe I'm overreacting. Mark probably isn't even interested in me."

"But it can't hurt to find out how we should handle these types of things."

"You're probably right," I conceded. "But I should probably talk to my dad." I groaned and flopped face-down onto my bed. "But that's going to be so embarrassing."

Lori came over and sat beside me. "Would it be easier if your mom were around?"

I rolled over and looked at her. "Honestly? Probably not. It's just not a subject that has come up. I mean, my mom talked to us about staying pure and all that, but that's all hypothetical when you aren't really interested in anybody, right? If I bring up the subject, I'm going to have to explain why I'm bringing up the subject. It's just embarrassing."

"Well, maybe at first. But sometimes you have to just jump in the water and get it over with. If you don't mind, can I call Megan? I'm wondering what my dating future is going to look like."

"Sure." I waved my hand towards the phone. "I guess I'll go downstairs and jump in the water." She was dialing before I even shut the door.

I trudged down the stairs trying to see if I could come up with a way to ask my dad about dating without actually admitting there was a guy I wanted to date. But I knew it was useless. Dad was bound to ask.

I found him reading a book, but at least he was alone. He looked up and took off his glasses when he saw me.

"Hey, Butterfly. Something on your mind?" He put his book aside and sat forward, motioning towards the ottoman. I sat down and tried to figure out what to say.

I knew he would sit there waiting patiently until I spit something out.

"How was your day?" I blurted.

He smiled and sat back in his chair. "Fine, Beka. But I doubt that's what you came down to ask me on New Year's Eve, a mere—" glancing at his watch, "—hour before you are going to a party."

"Okay. Here it is. Mom talked to me about, umm, you know, sex and stuff, but we never really talked about . . . I mean, I know that I'm not supposed to have sex before marriage and all that kind of stuff. But we never talked about the other stuff."

"The 'other' stuff? I'm not sure I know what you mean."

"Like, dating and boys and relationships and stuff." I pulled at a string on the sleeve of my sweater, trying not to make eye contact.

"Ohhh," was all he said for a minute. I almost had worked the string back through the small hole before he spoke again.

"Why are you bringing this up now? We don't exactly have very long to get into a discussion about this."

"I don't know." I shrugged but he narrowed his eyes at me. He knew I wasn't telling him everything.

"Well, there's this guy. But it's really nothing because I hardly know him and I don't know if he's interested in me anyway, but I guess I realized that even if he did ask me out I wouldn't know what to say because we hadn't really talked about it and I didn't know, well, I don't know what you expect of me." I ran out of breath as I finished. The water was cold, but at least it was out in the open.

"We do need to talk about this, but I'm not sure we have the time right now to do the subject justice. So let's talk about a few particulars tonight, and we'll come back to it when we have some more time. Does that sound okay?"

I nodded and breathed a sigh of relief. His calmness washed over me, and I could feel myself relax for the first time since I had walked downstairs.

"Your mom and I actually talked a lot about this as you girls grew older, and there were a couple of things that we agreed would govern our decisions in this area. The first thing is that the Bible is pretty clear about not being 'yoked' with unbelievers. Basically, that means that we really can't have a serious relationship with someone who does not know and follow God. So, if there is to be dating, which we'll get to in a minute, it can only be with a young man who loves the Lord."

"But how do you know that? I mean, I wasn't exactly being honest about God in my life. How do you really know if someone else is?"

"You shall know a tree by its fruit."

"Huh?" I grimaced.

"Well, you know a tree is an apple tree when there are apples on the tree, right? It's the same idea. It's why your mom and I suspected that your relationship with God wasn't okay—we didn't see any evidence of you really walking with God. When somebody really loves God and wants to follow Him, there's evidence. Things you see in their life that show you that's what's in their hearts. None of us will be perfect, but you will see true Christians trying to follow God."

"But what evidence am I supposed to see?"

"You don't know if this guy is a Christian, do you?"

"No," I admitted.

"Well, as you get to know God better and read the Bible, you'll start to see what I'm talking about. In the meantime, it's good to trust the people around you, like me, to help you make decisions. So if you want to get to know this guy better, then I will need to get to know him too."

"Seriously? That's going to be . . . uncomfortable."

"Don't worry about that now. We'll find a way to make it natural if it becomes necessary. In the meantime, watch and listen. You'll be surprised by what you notice when you ask God to help you see the truth."

"So, what else did you and Mom decide on?"

"We didn't want to make any blanket rules like 'No dating until such and such age' because all of you are different kids. So we really wanted to deal with each of you and each relationship you encounter individually. We wanted so much for God to guide you in the decisions you made and the relationships you forged that we felt it was important to model that for you. To show you that we wanted to be guided by God in making decisions that affect you. But that requires both of us being willing to let God guide us in this area—and it means we have to be able to talk about it. Which is why I'm so glad you came and asked tonight. It shows maturity, Beka. I'm proud of you."

I grinned in spite of myself. I didn't see it as a mature move—just a completely necessary one. As I walked back upstairs my head was still swirling a little bit.

What if God didn't want me to be with Mark? I also felt silly because I was acting like a relationship with Mark was even a possibility, when it probably wasn't. Did I want God to be in control of my love life?

I went back and forth and back and forth and finally realized something. I didn't have any control over what I was feeling, but I could make a decision to trust God. So I prayed. It probably wasn't a very good prayer, but I let God know that I wanted Him to be in control and that I would trust Him with my feelings for Mark and my future. I didn't feel any differently after I prayed. I wasn't sure if I was supposed to. But I did feel better about at least trying to do things right with God.

While we were getting ready I told Lori what I had prayed, and before long we were driving to Mark's house. I still had feelings for Mark, but I did notice that I wasn't as nervous about seeing him.

We arrived fashionably late. A lot of people were already there. Mark greeted us at the door.

"Beka! I'm so glad you could come." He smiled when he saw me.

"Hi, Mark. This is my friend Lori."

"Hi, Lori. Nice to meet you." He shook her hand and led us into the living room. He introduced us to about a dozen other people, and eventually we ended up settling onto the floor.

"Where do you know all these kids from?" I asked.

"Oh, they're, uh, mostly friends from church." He looked uncomfortable, but I didn't know why. Lori and I caught each other's eye when he said "church." I wondered. I knew enough to know that everybody who goes to church didn't necessarily follow God, but I found myself hoping. After all, there was no chance at all if Mark wasn't a Christian.

Mark's friends were nice. He touched base with us every so often as he went around playing host. Some people were watching a movie, some were playing pool in the basement, and some others were playing board games.

"I can see why you feel the way you do, Beka. He's really nice," Lori said when we had a moment alone.

"Yeah. I wonder though. A lot of these kids have been talking like they're saved. I wonder if Mark is a Christian. He seemed uncomfortable talking about church."

"I noticed that too. You see that dark-haired guy in the corner? His name is Brian, and he actually asked me if I knew Jesus. I told him that I just recently gave my life to Him, and he was thrilled. I may end up praying like you did before the end of this night." She smiled.

It was getting close to midnight when Mark came over to us.

"Beka, will you come for a walk with me?"

"Sure," I said nervously, glancing at Lori. She just smiled at me.

We went and got our coats and went into his backyard. It was a gorgeous night. Cold, but clear. And the stars were shining so brightly. I found myself awed by the fact that God had put them all there. We went and sat on top of the picnic table.

"I wanted to talk to you tonight," he began. I didn't know what to say so I just smiled and nodded.

"Last week, Gretchen made a few phone calls here hinting around about you."

I suddenly felt sick to my stomach. What had Gretchen told him?

I considered trying to defend myself immediately, but I couldn't formulate the words.

"Yeah. She was hinting around trying to find out how I felt about you. I didn't think it was any of her business how I felt about anybody, but I didn't know if she had said anything to you. Anyway, I wanted to talk to you about it tonight so there is no confusion. I hate these games that some girls play."

I still didn't know how to respond. It didn't sound like she had told him how I felt, but I didn't want to jump to any conclusions.

"Well, I know we haven't known each other very long. I wanted to be honest with you about the fact that

I am attracted to you. I would really like to get to know you better and spend time with you. But, well, I'm not allowed to date. My parents, they . . . well, I haven't always given them a reason to trust me, so the dating thing is on hold—indefinitely."

I was dumbfounded. Here he was, saying what I dreamed he'd say, and then he throws in the part about not dating. What did *that* mean? Since he was being honest, I decided it couldn't hurt to be honest right back.

"That's quite a bit to throw at a girl when you're sitting in the moonlight on New Year's Eve," I said as I tried to decide how to confess my feelings.

"I know. I'm sorry. I didn't want to pretend I don't like you, but I didn't want you to expect me to ask you out either."

"Well," I said as I kept my eyes on the ground, "I'm interested in you, too, but I don't think I understand. Why wouldn't your parents trust you?"

"That's a topic for another time, maybe. I made a promise to get my life together, and part of that is no dating and part of that is, well, church and stuff."

"Are you a Christian, Mark?" The question escaped my lips before I could stop it.

"Yes," he said slowly. "I've just blown it with God before. So even though I want to spend time with you, we can only be friends. It's about all I can handle."

"How long have you been a Christian?" I pressed. I was confused why nobody seemed to know.

"I became a believer when I was thirteen. Why?"

"Well, you seem awfully uncomfortable talking

about it for someone who has been saved almost four years. Are you ashamed to be a Christian?"

"What?" he asked, shocked.

"You seem ashamed of it. Nobody at school seems to know you are a Christian. You don't ever give anybody the real reason as to why you don't smoke and drink and swear and all those other things you don't do. Why don't you just admit that you choose not to do those things because of God? It seems to me you are taking all the credit for being Mr. Moral, when you should be telling people that you do what you do because of God."

He sat in silence for several minutes with his head resting in one of his hands. I thought I had made him angry, and I shifted nervously. I couldn't believe I had said all those things. I didn't even know I had been thinking all those things.

"Are you a Christian, Beka?" he asked, not moving.

"Yeah." I laughed. "For about three days I've been a Christian."

"Yet, you see right through me," he muttered.

We sat in silence for several more minutes. I finally decided I would have to break the silence.

"Look, it's fine with me if you want to be friends. I could use some more friends. And I am certainly not going to pressure you for any kind of commitment. I'm just getting started with God. I don't know yet how I feel about dating and relationships and all that, but I do know that I want God to be in control. And, for right now at least, that means I need to concentrate on my relationship with Him."

He looked up at me and smiled. The stars were so

bright; I could see every feature on his face. "You certainly are going to make it a lot harder," he said softly.

"What do you mean?"

"Well, it's going to be hard not to really fall for you. Especially after you stood up to me like that. That's a new one for me."

I smiled in spite of myself. My heart melted. I still didn't know what God was going to do with all the emotions, because they were very much present, despite our agreement to be friends.

We heard everybody inside yell suddenly, and we looked at each other.

"Happy New Year," he said as he reached over and hugged me.

"Happy New Year, Mark." I couldn't help enjoying the hug and closeness. We both lingered in the embrace for a few more moments. I was excited and scared all at the same time. What *would* my future hold? Would Mark be a part of it?

"Well, we better get back inside and celebrate with everybody. Besides, we probably shouldn't be hanging out in the moonlight too long." He grinned.

I reluctantly followed him back inside and found Lori and wished her a Happy New Year. She wanted to know what happened right then, but I told her quietly that I would fill her in on the way home. I tried to keep myself from floating too high over Mark. I kept reminding myself that we had agreed to be friends. But there was something so special about knowing that he cared about me.

We left soon after midnight so that we could be

home by my onetime 1 A.M. curfew. I filled Lori in on my moonlight conversation with Mark. She was really happy for me and seemed to think that it was really the best outcome that could have happened. I agreed. We stayed up talking for a long time. Apparently, she had really hit it off with Brian, so she was beginning to understand exactly how I was feeling. We prayed together before we went to sleep, asking God to be in control of our hearts. What a way to begin the New Year.

We slept late and got up and had a late breakfast with everybody. Anna and Lucy wanted to hear about the party, but mostly we talked about what we were looking forward to in the coming year. It was so nice to actually have things to look forward to.

I drove Lori home after we had helped clean up. She raved about my family once again. I filled her in on my Gabby dilemma while we were driving. We agreed that we would have to talk to Megan about how I should handle it. I was really looking forward to our weekly sessions with Megan. I felt really comfortable talking to her, and I was so glad that Lori was willing to share her.

I figured it must be hard. After all, Megan had just become her mother.

I stopped in for a few minutes with Lori to tell Megan about the party. I kind of wanted to talk her about Mark and the "friends" decision. I especially wanted to ask her if she thought there was any hope for anything else, but I didn't. I was happy with things as they were—no sense in messing with them yet. We all agreed to meet Wednesday after dinner for our first official meeting, since I had *Annie* rehearsals after school. I couldn't believe that school was going to start again. It felt like years had passed since I was there last.

On my way home, I got a sudden urge to go to the cemetery. I looked around for a florist that was open, but all I could find was a grocery store. I went in and bought some flowers and then drove to her grave site. I hadn't been there much. The tree next to her grave was spindly and bare. But instead of looking at it and being sad about how bare it was, I thought about how spring would come before long and it would look beautiful again.

I looked at the stone with her name and the dates of her life. I sat down after I put the flowers in the small vase at the base of the stone. I sat there for a long time, thinking about the last several months. My heart still ached for her. Maybe even more so because now I would have something special to share with her. Then again, I thought maybe I wouldn't have gotten to this point if she hadn't died. Maybe I would have gone on pretending. I knew there was no way to know for sure what might have been. All I did know is that despite the sadness, I had a second chance. I could start things anew. I felt stronger than I ever had before. Even knowing that I still had to deal with Gretchen and Gabby, even knowing that it would probably be difficult to make sure God had control over my heart with Mark, I felt confident. I felt like I had an ally. God was going to be there to help me through whatever I would have to face. I couldn't help wanting my mom back, and I doubted that feeling would ever really go away. But out of her death, I had a new life. And one day, I could count on seeing her again.

"Happy New Year, Mom. I love you."

FOR MORE INFORMATION:

www.becomingbeka.com

SINCE 1894, Moody Publishers has been dedicated to equip and motivate people to advance the cause of Christ by publishing evangelical Christian literature and other media for all ages, around the world. Because we are a ministry of the Moody Bible Institute of Chicago, a portion of the proceeds from the sale of this book go to train the next generation of Christian leaders.

If we may serve you in any way in your spiritual journey toward understanding Christ and the Christian life, please contact us at www.moodypublishers.com.

"All Scripture is God-breathed and is useful for teaching, rebuking, correcting and training in righteousness, so that the man of God may be thoroughly equipped for every good work."

—*2 TIMOTHY 3:16, 17*

MOODY
PUBLISHERS

THE NAME YOU CAN TRUST®

And The Bride Wore White

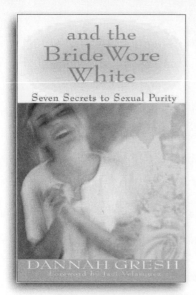

Only God has the power to enable us to remain sexually pure. Apart from Him the task is nearly impossible. Worldly passions engulf our youth, dragging them into a world for which they are unprepared and outside of God's will.

Dannah Gresh exposes the cultural lie about sex and presents the biblical truth regarding purity before marriage. She boils the truth down to seven easily understood secrets to sexual purity.

ISBN: 0-8024-8330-5

Secret Keeper

The practice of modesty is an intriguing and untapped power source. Let Dannah give you the facts of this power and show you how it really works.

Through Secret Keeper, *Dannah tells it like it is—full of truth and full of power! Definitely a must read for all young women.*

-Susie Shellenberger,
Editor, *Brio* Magazine

ISBN: 0-8024-3974-8

MOODY
PUBLISHERS

THE NAME YOU CAN TRUST.

1-800-678-6928 www.MoodyPublishers.com

THE MASQUERADE TEAM

ACQUIRING EDITOR:
Michele Straubel

COPY EDITOR:
Cheryl Dunlop

BACK COVER COPY:
The Livingstone Corporation

COVER DESIGN:
Barb Fisher, LeVan Fisher Design

INTERIOR DESIGN:
Ragont Design

PRINTING AND BINDING:
Dickinson Press Inc.

The typeface for the text of this book is
Aetna JY